# His Sensible Heart

A Touches of Austen Novel

## LEENIE BROWN

LEENIE B BOOKS
HALIFAX

Cover design by Leenie B Books. Images sourced from Deposit Photos and Period Images.

*His Sensible Heart* © 2020 Leenie Brown. All Rights Reserved, except where otherwise noted.

ISBN (print) 978-1-989410-77-6; (ebook) 978-1-989410-78-3

# Contents

*Dear Reader,*

This novel is part of my *Touches of Austen* Collection of Austenesque stories. These stories feature original characters and plots that have been touched in some way by the influence of Jane Austen and her novels.

In *His Sensible Heart*, there are a few nods to and mentions of *Sense and Sensibility*. For instance, the heroine is a sensible lady, much like Elinor Dashwood. She also has a less sensible sister. The gentleman who loves her does so to the detriment of his inheritance.

Along with the intentional nods to Miss Austen's work in this story, there may also be some which are purely serendipitous, and, then, there is one special nod in the description and actions of Miles's tutor to a character from *Pride and Prejudice* for the true lover of Jane Austen to discover.

If you would like to share your observations

about which elements you thought were Austen-inspired, you can do that in my *Touches of Austen Readers Group* on Facebook.

Happy Reading!

# Chapter 1

The clock on the bookshelf behind Miles Chapman marked the time with a loud and steady rhythm while he sat in the oppressive stillness of the room, waiting to hear his fate. The desires of his heart along with the deviousness of his father lay open before the gentleman whose daughter Miles wished to marry. As the minutes ticked away, he prayed his candidness was enough to earn him some favour.

Mr. Wesley's chin rested on his clasped hands, propped up by his elbows on the large mahogany desk that stood between him and Miles. He tipped his head as his quiet scrutiny continued. Finally, after a torturous number of minutes, Mr. Wesley lifted his head and spoke.

"While I find it admirable that you have severed your ties with your father, Mr. Chapman, you must understand that your ability to provide for my daughter is a grave concern to me." Mr. Wesley leaned back in his chair.

"But the rumours, sir," Miles pleaded, earning him a sympathetic smile, an expression which only meant one thing – his heart, which lay open and vulnerable, was about to be crushed.

"That gossip is likely why Charlotte has given you permission to speak to me. She is a sensible girl who is not unaware of the damage the stories you claim are being spread will bring." Mr. Wesley folded his hands across his abdomen as if there was nothing wrong in all the world. "I have not heard any rumours, but if there are some, I am not afraid to face them."

"Are you refusing my offer?" Miles's heartbeat echoed in his ears. The happy picture of a future with Charlotte at his side began to fray at the edges and threatened to dissolve.

Mr. Wesley shrugged. "I am neither refusing nor accepting. I am postponing."

"Postponing?" How did one postpone an offer of marriage, and did that mean there was hope for Miles to claim the lady who had captured his heart, or was the man just prolonging his agony, much like a cat playing with a mouse which would eventually become its dinner?

"I know extraordinarily little about you, Mr. Chapman, and the little which I have heard does you no favours. It was, after all, Charlotte's desire to escape your constant attention that reinforced her decision to visit her grandparents." He rose from his chair and moved to stand behind it. "You are, in her words, an arrogant popinjay who is more fascinated with his looks and status than anything else."

The words hit Miles like a mirror shattering over his head in a row with the boys. However, that incident had not drawn blood the way Mr. Wesley's words made his pride bleed.

"Do you deny it?" Mr. Wesley asked.

Miles shook his head. "I cannot. Miss Wesley is an astute judge of character. I have been encouraged all my life to be just like my father." He released a breath. "And your daughter's description fits my father perfectly, though I would add to it a few more descriptors about his callous cruelty – to which, by the by, I have never aspired." What he would give at this moment to have had any other father!

"The sins of the fathers," Mr. Wesley muttered with a look of pity for Miles. "I will give you one year, young man, to put your affairs in order and to prove yourself worthy of my daughter."

Miles's eyebrows flew up to where his longish blond hair fell over his forehead. "A year?" That was a dreadfully long time to be uncertain of one's future, was it not?

"Both you and my Charlotte are excessively young. You have not even earned your bachelor's. You have admitted to being of what I would consider questionable character, for, to my way of thinking, any man who thinks more of his looks than his studies or his fellow travellers on this earth is lacking in integrity. You have also acknowledged that your father is a fearsome and cruel man, and I am not certain I wish to have my daughter tied to him in any fashion. Added to these things, is the fact that you are newly cut-off from your father. When your allowance is gone, will your resolve remain?"

"Yes." Miles rose quickly from his chair. "I will never be reconciled to my father."

"I require proof," Mr. Wesley said flatly. "While you have professed your love for Charlotte, I am of the belief that my daughter does not love you. I will not let her enter a marriage of unequal affections. Therefore, you have a year to prove yourself and to earn her good opinion. Provided she will allow it, I will permit you to call on her."

"How can I call on her when, eventually, I am in Bath, and she is here?" Oxfordshire was not a short jaunt from Bath, and he only had one more term – a few months – at school. Then, he would have to take up his position as a research assistant and aide to Mr. Norman.

"You may correspond with her, and if there is a wish for it on her part, she will be permitted to travel to Bath to visit her grandparents." He crossed to the door to his study. "She returns to us on Wednesday. We will expect you to join us for dinner on Saturday next. Use your week to see to your studies. I know that is not how most gentlemen commoners approach their time at Oxford, but that is how I expect someone intent upon winning my approval to conduct himself."

"Yes, sir." At least, he was not completely without hope.

"I am sorry you have lost your father, such that

he was," Mr. Wesley said before Miles exited the room.

Miles gave a sharp nod of his head. It was more than just his father that he had lost. He had lost nearly all his family, as well as his inheritance. While he did not regret his decision, he did feel like donning mourning clothes.

"I am here if you need anything," Mr. Wesley offered.

The kindness in the man's eyes caused Miles to pause before returning his appreciation of the offer. Mr. Wesley's expression was one that he had never seen in his own father's eyes. He had witnessed the kindness with which some of his friends had been treated by their fathers, but until this moment, he had not felt the warmth that such a thing could bring to a soul in quite the way he had just experienced it. While Mr. Wesley was not clapping him on the shoulder and welcoming him to the family, he was also not throwing him out. It was almost as if the man wished for Miles to succeed in the quest placed before him.

Standing on the drive next to his carriage, Miles turned halfway and looked back at the flat façade of the Wesleys' home with its three rows of symmetrical windows. Had anyone ever left the fate of his welcome to his own efforts?

He climbed into his curricle and took up the reins.

Mr. Norman seemed the sort to allow Miles to prove his worth, but Mr. Norman was not the father of the prettiest lady Miles had ever met. Therefore, his acceptance and expectations held a different weight. They were the masters of his future career, not the future of his heart.

"Walk on."

He would have to make certain he could keep his carriage and horses on whatever money his father sent him. There was no other way to call on Charlotte but to drive. Her home was too far from his own lodgings for him to walk. He sighed. Perhaps he could petition his aunt if needed, though he truly did not wish to do so. Deep within him, there was a desire to prove himself by himself. It was the same desire, though arguably altered in its direction, which had driven him to perform to his father's satisfaction – and just look at how well he had succeeded there until he had found something far greater in value than the accolade of a father who only truly cared about the success of his son because of how it reflected on him. Compared to the value of Sir Allen's own figure in society, his son – nay all his children – meant extraordinarily little.

How had he conformed to such a lowly position as being the accessory to his father's appearance?

At the end of the driveway, Miles turned his carriage unto the road which would take him to his accommodations. He would have an hour to consider his former behaviour and how he could change it before he would draw near to his apartment.

And consider it, he did. For twenty minutes he berated himself for his self-absorbed arrogance. Then, for the next fifteen minutes, he reviewed his interactions with Charlotte. It was not a pretty reviewal. He had inserted himself in her group whenever he had seen her. He had not waited to be invited. He had not even requested permission to join her. He had just assumed that he would be welcomed, for how could anyone not wish for his presence? And with that thought in mind, he returned to scolding himself for his conceit.

"Do you realize what an idiot I am?" He asked the fellow who met him as he walked from where his horses and carriage were stabled toward the block of rooms that they both called home.

"You may need to clarify in what sense I am to be considering your idiot-ness." Miles's long-time friend, Thomas Green, answered with a laugh.

Miles shook his head and chuckled. "I am a pompous imbecile, Tom. In fact, I am such a bombastic buffoon, that if there were a book in the Bodleian about such fools, mine would be the image inscribed as an illustration."

"Am I to understand, from the colourful image you are painting of yourself, that your visit with a certain lady's father did not go well?"

"No, it did not go well. However, it did not go completely poorly either." He took note of his friend's expression. "That is precisely how I have been feeling – turned about and set on my head." He stopped walking and stood at the bottom of the staircase which would take him to his apartment. "Or perhaps, I have finally been stood right side up and am so unaccustomed to it that I feel out of sorts."

That was likely it. His father had never stood him up properly. Indeed, his father likely did not know what it was to stand upright. He climbed the stairs behind his friend.

"I have a year."

"For what?" Tom asked over his shoulder.

"To complete my schooling and convince Miss Wesley that I am not the sort of fellow she should run from, but rather the sort she should run to."

"She still is not favourably inclined towards you, is she?"

"Not at all, according to her father." And she had not been pleased to see him when he arrived in Bath. Nor had she seemed overly saddened by his leaving her in Bath with her grandparents while he returned to Oxford. Perhaps, Mr. Wesley was correct.

"Not even with your offer to save her reputation?"

"Not even then." Miles pushed open the door to his rooms.

"Is she worth it?" Tom asked as he followed Miles into the sitting room. "You have given up a great deal for her already, and if she is not, at least, somewhat impressed by your sacrifices on her behalf, do you think she merits the effort it will require to convince her that you are a worthy prospect?"

Miles removed his jacket and unbuttoned his waistcoat before dropping into a chair. "I should have given up all I had when I heard what my father did to my sister."

"You were sixteen." Tom took the chair next to Miles.

Miles shook his head. "How did I not see how vile he is?"

Tom shrugged. "Your allowance was blindingly good."

A bitter laugh escaped Miles. "And now I wish I had been more frugal and less frivolous with it."

"What son of a wealthy father is not careless when he is young?"

Miles leveled a pointed look at his friend. "You, for one."

Tom chuckled. "My father was not so generous as yours. I have had to be careful."

"We are opposites, are we not?" Miles said. "You are sensible, and I am not."

"And yet, we make a good pair."

Miles nodded, leaned his head against the back of his chair, and looked up at the ceiling. "Belle was always my favorite sister. She still is, and not just because her husband is going to give me a position. She is practical, and she liked learning about how to care for wounds and illnesses as much as I did." He smiled. "I used to love telling her silly stories just to hear her laugh." He sighed. "It became harder to do after Father did what he did to her and Mr. Norman." He turned his head to look at Tom. "You realize, of course, that this is privileged information, and that if you share that I was being maudlin, there are a few stories I could tell about you."

Tom laughed. "When have I ever shared your secrets?"

"Never, but..." Miles blew out a breath. "Life is not what it was. I find I need reassurance that you have not changed."

"I have not changed," Tom assured him. "I am still the annoying friend who shall be at your door, demanding you join me in partaking of the learning on offer, far earlier than you wish for me to be." He grew serious. "The question regarding Miss Wesley remains unanswered. Is she worth it?"

"Suffice it to say, my friend, that I fully intend to allow you to elaborate on the joys of learning as we go to the library tomorrow, for surely, there must be some discourse or essay that wants preparation."

# Chapter 2

Charlotte Wesley carefully clicked the door to her bedroom closed and stole down the stairs in her stocking feet. She longed for a solitary stroll in the walled garden before eating breakfast or having a meeting with her father.

Last evening, upon her return from Bath, nothing had been said about Mr. Chapman except to say that he had called and that her father would speak to her in the morning. Instead, the evening had been filled with inquiries about her grandparents and her time in Bath.

She sank down on the bottom step of the staircase to put on her boots. The suspense of waiting to know her fate was so great that it not only filled her mind during her waking hours, it had also begun to paint her dreams.

"Did you sleep well?"

The question drew a startled squeak from Charlotte.

"I did not mean to frighten you," her father said as he sat down next to her. "Are you still in the habit of sneaking out in the mornings?"

"Of course." She had been slipping out to the garden for a morning stroll since she was ten and her father had said it was allowed. "It is still the best time of the day to clear one's mind and order one's thoughts before duties must be attended to."

"I have always thought so myself," her father replied. "And what might be troubling your mind this morning, my daughter?"

Charlotte peeked up at him from where she was bent tying her boot. "Do you truly wonder?"

He shook his head. "No, I had just hoped to hear you admit that a certain young man is on your mind."

She gave her laces one final tug and tied them in a bow before sitting up and turning toward her father. "How can Mr. Chapman not be on my mind?"

"Is it a happy ponderance or one which grieves you?"

That was a most excellent question. One to

which she had no answer, so instead of replying, she shrugged.

"Come." Her father stood and held his hand out to her. "I will escort you on your walk because sometimes it helps to have someone to help sort out the knots of tangled thoughts."

Apparently, the solitary stroll for which she longed was not to be. She sighed inwardly before placing her hand in her father's and allowing him to help her to her feet. Once her hand was securely tucked around his arm, the two walked leisurely down the hall, through the sitting room, and out the garden door.

The spring air which greeted them was fresh and crisp, but the scarcity of clouds in the sky and the cheerfulness of the sun's brightness spoke of a warm, clear day ahead. The trills and chirps of the birds in the trees seemed to confirm the assessment that today was going to be a beautiful May day.

"Did you sleep well?" her father repeated the question, which had startled her earlier, when they were several yards away from the house.

"Mostly, but to be truthful, I have not slept overly well for the past week."

"And why would that be?"

She hated to admit the reason, for it did not sound at all like her. "I was troubled at the thought of coming home."

She had always loved her home, but now, knowing that there were rumours swirling about her and that Mr. Chapman had spoken to her father, home had become a place of unrest rather than solace.

"Much has taken place. It is quite normal for you to feel unsettled about things and how they lie."

Normal it may be, but welcome it was not. Perhaps if she were to just discover what the future held, then she might be able to order her mind to accept it. "How do they lie? Am I to be Mrs. Chapman?"

"Do you wish to be?"

"My wishes have very little to do with what must happen."

It was the best answer she could give her father, for her heart was as conflicted now about Mr. Chapman as it had been six weeks ago when she had left for Bath. He was charming when he was not being arrogant, but he was so often arrogant that it caused his alluring smile and infectious humor to feel like it was something she should not enjoy. Simply put, she found him enticing and that felt wrong. He was not the sort of gentleman to whom she had ever aspired to be connected.

"I will not force you to marry Mr. Chapman if you do not wish to do so."

They stopped in front of the fountain that stood in the middle of the garden. Paths led to the right and left, as well as continuing in the direction they were going on the other side of the pond in which the fountain stood.

"Neither your mother nor I have heard any rumours such as those about which you wrote to us, and I have not heard Louisa mention any odd looks when she and your mother were in town last. It is possible that whatever tales might have been started died out almost as quickly as they began."

"Or they will not erupt into a furor until the object of ridicule has returned." She cringed at the thought. All those years of being exactly what she was expected to be – undone in an instant and through no fault of her own. She had always thought that if anyone were to be the source of rumours in their family, it would be her younger sister, for Louisa was the more reckless and care-free Miss Wesley.

"I suppose we will discover that soon enough," her father agreed.

"Unless I never go to town again."

"That does not seem very sensible, now does it?"

It most certainly did not. It sounded dramatic and like something Louisa would say. However, at the moment, Charlotte felt a great deal more like acting as her sister would than acting as she knew she should.

"Why should I be sensible? It has not prevented this..." her free hand flew around in a circle in the air as if indicating the whole world, "...mess."

Her father sighed. "You would not know how to be anything but sensible, my dear. You are the only child I have ever heard of who straightened the nursery without being told to do so. Sensibility is woven into who you are. Do you wish to go to the right or the left?"

"I wish to sit and toss petals in the pond." She also felt like stamping her foot and pouting, but she could not quite bring herself to act so.

He chuckled. "We will sit, but I believe the flowers will stay intact." He scooped a handful of pebbles from the border of the walkway. "You may cast these into the water. They make a far more satisfying splash." He sat with her on the small wall that was the border of the pond. "And while you throw pebbles, I will tell you how I see your future."

The pebble she held between her fingers did not leave them. "Is it decided then?"

Part of her wanted to mourn the loss of what could have been – a few years of dancing, theatre, drives, and calls, during which she would find the perfect sensible husband and settle into a quiet life at his estate – while another portion of her wanted to sigh in relief, for it knew she could indulge her admiration of Mr. Chapman without it feeling wrong, since admiring him would be expected of his future wife.

"No."

Her eyes grew wide. "It is not? Did you refuse Mr. Chapman?" Why did she feel panic welling within her at the thought?

"No."

"Father!" The smile he wore was far too amused. "Must you torment me?"

He laughed. "Just a little. It builds tolerance in one who is as sensible as you."

"I am not certain it does."

He picked up a pebble from the pile that lay

between them and tossed it into the water. "I have postponed Mr. Chapman's offer."

"Postponed?" How did one postpone an offer of marriage? Did one not just accept or deny?

"Yes, postponed. I have given him a year to prove he can provide for you as you deserve."

"He has no estate, and a year will not alter that fact."

"No, he does not have an estate, but neither did my great-grandfather. And yet, look at where we sit now. Just because a gentleman does not have an estate does not mean he will never have one. Nor does it mean he cannot provide a comfortable home and a good life for his wife and children. If a man is diligent, much can be accomplished."

And that was the problem. "Mr. Chapman is not diligent."

"He will be if he wishes to marry you." Her father's tone brooked no argument. Charlotte knew that when he used that tone, what he said would not change.

"I have instructed him to spend this week attending to his studies, and when he comes to dinner on Saturday, I shall discover if he has done as requested." His lips tipped up on the right side as he tossed another pebble in the pond. "There is something about him that I like, which makes no sense since I have only just met him and what I have heard about him from you has not been favourable."

"You like him?" The thought was both surprising and reassuring. Her father was the most sensible man she knew, and if he could be uncertain about liking Mr. Chapman, then perhaps her uncertainty was not so very strange after all.

"I do. However, that does not mean he is worthy of my daughter."

And she was back to feeling muddled.

"We are down to three pebbles. Do you wish to walk further, or would you prefer to tell me all you know about Mr. Norman over a cup of coffee?"

Charlotte wrinkled her nose. "Coffee is abominable."

Her father chuckled. "You may have chocolate."

"May I not just sit here for a while longer?"

Her father gave her a long look before rising. "I suppose you may, but I do wish to know your thoughts on Mr. Norman. Your grandfather has sung his praises as a physician, but do you think he will be a good man for whom to work?"

Charlotte nodded. "He called on me while I was in Bath."

"Your grandfather told me about that and how it did not work out in your favour."

"He is the best gentleman – kind, intelligent, sensible –" and she had liked him, though not enough to hope he would ask her to marry him, "but he was in love with Miss Chapman and had been for years. They are so happy now." She could not help the sigh and smile that the thought of Mr. Norman and Miss Chapman being reunited brought to her. Theirs was a love story that she would remember and share someday with her own daughter.

"Is Miss Chapman like her brother?"

"No. She is his opposite."

"He thinks very highly of her."

"I cannot see how anyone could think any other way about her."

Miss Chapman, now Mrs. Norman, was beautiful from the bottom of her feet to the top of her cap. She shone with compassion, and she carried herself with grace. Charlotte had hoped that, if she were to be told to stay in Bath rather than coming home, she and Mrs. Norman would become friends. She had also hoped to become friends with Mrs. Blakesley.

She stood and took her father's arm. She could sit and confuse herself about Mr. Chapman later. Right now, she wanted to tell her father about her acquaintances in Bath.

"Mr. Norman's dearest friend is Mr. Blakesley."

"And who is Mr. Blakesley?"

"Why Mrs. Blakesley's husband, of course." She laughed at her father's sigh. "He is a gentleman of good standing in Bath who owns an estate, as well as several other homes which he leases to those who frequent Bath at various times of the year."

"Ah," her father sighed the word contentedly, "an industrious fellow."

"Very, and he is Mr. Norman's dearest friend."

"I see. You mean to illustrate to me that Mr. Norman is also industrious."

"He had to be. His career was nearly ruined by Miss Chapman's father."

Her father nodded. "I know. Mr. Chapman told me the whole sordid story."

"Mr. Norman is now amongst the most highly regarded in his profession, which is why Mr. Chapman wishes to work with him. He says he will be able to learn a lot from Mr. Norman." That was something which had surprised her because she had not thought Mr. Chapman to be fond of any sort of learning, yet he said he was.

"And what do you think?"

"I think Mr. Norman is knowledgeable; therefore, I do not doubt that one could learn a great deal from him if one were inclined to do so." And therein lay the issue. She doubted Mr. Chapman. She doubted his desire to learn, she doubted his contentment with being a research assistant when he had been a gentleman of leisure for so long, but, most importantly, she doubted his attachment to her.

# Chapter 3

Miles turned his carriage into the drive that would lead him to the Wesleys' front door. It was not a long drive nor was it winding. It was, in fact, sensibly positioned to make the approach direct, yet situated in such a way that was not off-putting to the person who wished for a moment to admire the front façade of the home to which it led.

Miles wished it were a more twisting and turning approach instead of the gentle sweep that it was, for he could use a moment to steady his nerves. Tonight's soiree was no simple dinner party. Tonight, he would give an account of his week to Mr. Wesley in hopes that the man would continue to consider Miles's offer to marry his daughter.

Despite the seemingly never-ending tedium of the week, he had met Mr. Wesley's demands, for Charlotte was worth the drudgery. For her, he had spent a full week of his break with Tom in the library or in his room, introducing himself to the wide array of things he would need to know. He had thought it better to assess the requirements, and, thereby, determine which would be most challenging. Then, he would know where best to focus his efforts.

"I do not know why I had to come with you."

"I told you, Tom. I need you to vouchsafe for me that I applied myself to my studies." Miles doubted that his own word regarding his studies would hold very much weight with Mr. Wesley. Therefore, he had written on Wednesday and asked if he could bring his friend with him tonight.

"How will Mr. Wesley know to trust me? I could be some fool you paid to say whatever you wished to be said."

Miles blew out an exasperated breath. Why would Mr. Wesley not trust Tom was the better question. No one would ever think Tom was just some fool. "I do not know why you are grumbling so. You will get a fine meal and a night of entertainment for your efforts."

"I could have both of those things at The Drunken Boar."

Miles turned his best, most fetching smile on his friend, for he knew such an expression would annoy his grousing friend. "But you would not have had my company."

"You overestimate my desire for your company, old friend, and I doubt I will be anywhere near your thoughts once you are in the presence of Miss Wesley."

"She has parents and a sister, and from what I could tell on my first visit, the house is well-staffed. I am certain someone can either entertain or employ you."

Tom was an excessively studious and intelligent fellow. There was positively no way that Mr. Wesley would not believe a report from the likes of Tom, and Miles was certain that Tom knew it. However, while Tom was, in most circumstances, decidedly confident, he was not the overly social sort. He kept to his group of friends. Occasionally, that group of friends would pull him along to some new setting, but he never went along without protesting the situation.

Miles drew the carriage to a stop, but, before relinquishing his reins to the groomsman who was quick to come to Miles's side, he turned to his friend. "Look, Tom, I know you do not like first meetings, but I am telling you that you will enjoy Mr. Wesley. I could tell from the moment I met the man that you and he are alike."

One of Tom's eyebrows cocked in disbelief.

"I mean it, and I am almost entirely certain of my assessment."

"How very reassuring," Tom said dryly.

Miles studied his friend who was still looking mulish and said the one thing that he knew Tom would not argue against. "I need you."

Tom closed his eyes and expelled a great sigh. "You seem a very capable sort of fellow to me."

"And I will do my best to make your introduction easy, just like I always do."

"Very well, I shall get out of the carriage and accompany you on your call."

Miles tossed the reins he held to the waiting groomsman and hopped down. Then, after straightening his coat, he joined Tom where he was standing in front of the Wesleys' house.

"Do try to be civil," Miles whispered before stepping towards what was to be an examination of his worthiness.

"When am I ever not civil?"

"When you think no one can hear you." There were many times when Tom would mutter under his breath about something to which he had taken exception while in company. Most times, the mutterings were done in a low enough voice so that only those next to Tom would hear them. The trouble came when Tom forgot his surroundings.

"Do you remember when you forgot that Mrs. Clarkson was sitting next to you, and you had to comment on the musical performance?"

Tom's expression pinched. Apparently, he did remember how unhappy Mrs. Clarkson had been to hear Tom compare the lady singing with a cat whose tail had been stepped on.

"Right. I will do my best." He hurried after Miles. "In my defense, I did not realize it was Mrs. Clarkson's niece who was singing."

"That is why it is best to keep one's disapproval to one's self until after one has left the musicale."

"But she was dreadful," Tom protested.

"I am not disagreeing."

The door before them opened.

"Mr. Chapman and Mr. Green," Miles said by way of introduction.

"You are punctual." Mr. Wesley, who was standing just behind his butler, tucked his watch into his pocket.

"Except when he wishes to be fashionably late," Tom muttered.

This was why Miles had reminded him to be civil. Apparently, trying to do his best to be civil did not extend to his friend.

"Which is a behaviour that I have put in the past," Miles said in response to Mr. Wesley's raised eyebrows. "Mr. Wesley, this is my good friend, Mr. Thomas Green. Tom, Mr. Wesley."

"It is a pleasure to meet you, Mr. Green."

"Likewise."

"Mr. Chapman mentioned in his letter that you have been studying together."

"Indeed, we have been. For the most part, it has been pleasant to have company while reading in the library."

Mr. Wesley's eyes sparkled with the same sort of quick-witted amusement Miles had always found delightful in Charlotte's expression when he had watched her from afar. The fact that she never wore that look when he approached her, but had rather favoured an expression of mild annoyance in his presence, should have been a clue to Miles that he was not admired by the lady. However, it had not been, because he had been an arrogant dandy who had never considered that a young lady would not wish for his presence.

"And what made the unpleasant part unpleasant?" Mr. Wesley asked.

Miles stifled a groan. He had brought Tom with him to help him make a good impression on Mr. Wesley and so far, that plan was falling apart in great pieces – and they had only just entered the house and been divested of their outerwear!

"The questions." It was more of a moan than a comment. "So many questions."

"Which," Miles hastily inserted, "comes from not attending lectures as I should have." If all his folly was to be aired, he was going to air part of it. He did not want Mr. Wesley to think he was attempting to hide his previously poor behaviour.

"Has Mr. Chapman been faithful to his time with you?" Mr. Wesley asked Tom with no more than a small smile of approval for Miles's confession of fault.

"He has."

"I am happy to hear it. He strikes me as a fellow with a good amount of potential."

"I could not agree with you more. If only he would believe it."

Had they forgotten he was even there? Miles half expected them to stroll off arm in arm without him in a moment. They really were two of a kind and his assessment that they would get on well appeared to be accurate.

"I suspect I know why he does not." Mr. Wesley turned his attention back to Miles. "I was worried at first that you would bring some fellow with you who would say whatever you wished him to say so that I would believe you had been studying whether you had been or not. However, your friend does not seem to be that sort of gentleman."

"He never has been, though, at present, I wish he were less forward with his honesty."

Mr. Wesley chuckled. "His honesty has helped you pass this first test. I would not despair of it too much. You will have to tell me which part of your studies this week you enjoyed most." He motioned for them to join him in walking down the corridor.

"Truthfully, I enjoyed my friend's companionship the most."

"None of the subjects?"

"No, there was nothing which truly interested me in any of what we were studying."

"That is not true," Tom said. "The apostle Luke and writer of the third gospel was a physician. You did find that bit of information interesting."

That was true. "But that is just one fact. It was not a significant portion of our studies."

"Perhaps not, but it was a point of interest."

"There were no other points of interest?" Mr. Wesley asked.

Miles shook his head. "Sadly, no. I wish there were for it would make studying a great deal easier."

"Perhaps as you get into your subjects further," Mr. Wesley said hopefully. "If you have not been attending lectures as you should, then, it is natural for one to be overwhelmed and confused by the material before him. However, that does not have to remain as it is."

"I hope you are correct, sir." For if Miles could not find a hint of fascination with the material he was required to know, it was going to be a dreadfully distasteful final term.

They stood at the door to a drawing room which was decorated in several peaceful shades of blue and accented with white and a touch of yellow here and there. His father would most likely approve of the décor, though he might find it to be a trifle understatedly elegant. Not that it mattered what his father thought. He needed to remember that. His opinion did not have to reflect that of his father's any longer, which was excellent in this case, for Miles whole-heartedly approved of the décor.

"Gentlemen, allow me to make the proper introductions," Mr. Wesley said as he led them into the room.

All three Wesley ladies were petite with fair skin and blonde hair. Mrs. Wesley, whom Miles had met before, had the same pleasant smile that Charlotte did, while Miss Louisa, whom he had seen but not yet met, wore a smile which was slightly more amused than pleasant. If Miles were to place a bet on it, which would require him to still have the assurance of his allowance, which he did not, he would have to say that Miss Louisa Wesley was a trifle less sensible than her older sister, and from the way she was peeking up at Tom through her lashes, he would also say that she was more adept at flirting than Charlotte was.

"Our meal will be ready shortly," Mrs. Wesley assured them. "My husband will pour you something to drink while we wait. Please be seated."

Miles thanked her and looked at Tom. "Pick a seat," he whispered.

"Me?"

Miles gave one nod of his head. He had inserted himself in Miss Wesley's group at every event where he had seen her previously. He was not about to continue that practice now, nor did he want to appear too eager.

"You may sit with us," Miss Louisa offered. "Mr. Green." She motioned to the chair which was positioned at her end of the couch on which she sat with Charlotte. "You may sit by me, and Mr. Chapman can sit by Lottie."

"A perfect arrangement," Mrs. Wesley agreed with alacrity.

"Is it?" Miles asked Charlotte as he took a seat in the chair next to her. He had seen the displeased glance she had directed at her sister. It was not a promising start.

"Perfect may not be the correct word," Charlotte replied.

She looked nervous, nearly as nervous as he felt.

He rubbed his hands on his breeches. Nervous was not something Miles felt very often. Relaxed and unconcerned where his normal ways of being.

"I am happy you arrived home safely from Bath."

"Thank you. It was not a difficult journey."

"That is good."

At a loss for words was also something which was not normal for Miles, and yet, here he was with nothing coming to his mind to say.

"I understand from my father that you have been studying this week."

"I have. Tom, er, Mr. Green, has been helping me get things sorted."

"That is kind of him. He must be a good friend."

"He is." Miles could not help but smile at that. He had no better friend than Tom. In fact, he was not certain a better friend could be found. "We have been friends for these past three years, but it seems we have known each other longer. He is very much the sort of friend one wishes to make and keep."

Interest registered in Charlotte's eyes and her attention turned to Tom. "Is he, indeed? What makes him so?"

Perhaps he should not have brought Tom with

him, for the lady whom Miles was supposed to be charming seemed far more interested in Tom than she did in Miles.

"He is steady."

"Steady?" Her tone was bemused.

"Sensible, diligent, loyal." It irritated Miles to have to list his friend's best qualities to Charlotte. "He is honestly just a good man." He blew out a breath. "The opposite of me," he added in not quite a whisper but almost.

Her attention shifted back to him. "Surely Mr. Green is not all good. Everyone has some flaw."

"Do you? For I do not see it."

Her cheeks grew rosy, but her eyes did not move from his. "We are not speaking about me. We are talking about what flaws your friend might have."

Other than being far more fascinating to both Wesley sisters than he himself was? Miles shook his head. "He can be surly when he does not wish to do something, and I do not mean mildly so. He grouses and grumbles, and occasionally pouts – though he would likely call it a scowl and not a pout. He actually argued in the carriage with me for the majority of our journey tonight."

"He did not want to come?" Her eyes were wide.

"I am only telling this to you because you have asked, and I believe you would not do him any harm with the information."

"Of course, I would not," she inserted as she eagerly leaned towards him.

"He finds new social venues to be..."

"Frightening?" she asked when he paused.

"Anxiety inducing, but only until he is there. Then, after I have introduced him, he relaxes. So, you can see why I say he is just simply a good man."

Her brow furrowed. "I can?"

Miles nodded. "I did not have to tie him up and toss him into my carriage in order for him to accompany me. He came, despite his unease, just because I requested it of him."

Her features softened, and a genuine smile graced both her lips and her eyes. "He seems relaxed now, which seems to say you are not completely his opposite and that there might be some good in you."

She thought he might be good? That was promising was it not? "How so?"

"You must have introduced him well if he is so at ease as he appears."

"I gave him something about which he could

grumble. Not that it was planned. He just kind of found one of my many flaws about which to mutter."

"Oh," she looked confused.

"Thank you."

"For what?"

"For attempting to make me not appear so poorly as I know I might when compared to Tom."

Her mouth fell open and then closed. "Are you always so hard on yourself?" Her tone was one of utter bewilderment, and he could not blame her. Until now, she had only seen his self-absorbed arsedness.

Miles laughed. "No. I used to be happily blind to my imperfections until... well... until I saw my father through fresh eyes. Thanks to you."

# Chapter 4

The idea of being the cause of the illumination of Mr. Chapman's mind to the folly of his behaviour might have been a welcome thought to Charlotte if she had spoken to him on the subject, and he, going away, had thought on her words and resolved to correct his errors. However, since she was merely the object of his father's monstrous actions and, for that reason, the light which shone into the dull corners of a mind too given to its own self-aggrandizement, being the source of Mr. Chapman's enlightenment was anything but welcome. She almost would have rather had Mr. Chapman remain ignorantly arrogant.

"I am not certain I wish to be thanked for such a service," she said to him with a smile which she hoped was light and pleasant.

"Of course," he muttered. "Forgive me." He gave

a nod of his head and fell silent while his eyes shifted to watch his friend.

This melancholy, silent version of Mr. Chapman was quite unsettling. While Charlotte was happy that he was not crowing about himself, she could not help but miss some of the liveliness which had always animated his features on each of the other times when they had met. Even in Bath, when he had called upon her and explained to her all that his father was and the plans he had to see that she was given a happy future, his eyes had not held the sadness that resided in them at present.

"We have had fine weather for this time of year," she said to break the uncomfortable silence that hung between them.

One corner of his mouth tipped up. "Yes, it has only rained three days this week." His tone was teasing, which she found hopeful.

"The garden seemed to welcome the refreshment even if I was not delighted by staying indoors."

There, that turned his eyes back to her with some interest. "Do you enjoy nature?"

"Very much so. I think it is the best place to be when one wishes to contemplate deeply."

"You enjoy it for thinking?" His eyebrows were raised in astonishment.

"Indeed, I do."

"Perhaps I should consider that for studying. I find that the library, much like the lecture hall, is excellent for wishing to sleep." He laughed lightly.

"I cannot believe it is always so. Did you not tell me that you enjoyed research and writing?"

"I do," he assured her with alacrity. "However, that is when the topic is of my choosing and of great interest to me. I fear that the classics are not so interesting as, say, studies on vaccination or how Mr. Norman has used exercise to help his patients with various ailments."

"My grandfather bemoans Mr. Norman's pre-scribed foul contraption."

His brow furrowed. "A chamber horse, was it not?"

"That is it precisely." How her grandfather had grumbled each day about riding it! But no matter the amount of grumbling that wafted around the breakfast room, he never took his meal without first having bounced the sleep out of his system.

"They are not so bad."

"I quite agree."

He blinked. "Have you..." He seemed embarrassed to continue his question.

"I have ridden it, for I wished to know how it worked." Both her grandfather and her grandmother had encouraged her to give it a try when she first began asking about it. Learning was not just something her father encouraged.

"Oh." He seemed surprised but not unhappily so.

"I like riding nearly as much as I like walking, and if I suffered from the stiff joints my grandfather does, I would welcome the diversion and relief a chamber horse could give me since riding a real horse when one has such an ailment is not always easy, nor is it advisable."

A genuine smile lit his face. "I thought the same when I first gave a chamber horse a go. Did you try a Bath Oliver biscuit or two?"

Her brow furrowed. That seemed an odd question to ask and not at all related to taking exercise.

"I did," she answered.

"I only ask," he said, "because our discussion of the chamber horse and stiff joints put me in the mind of them."

"How?" They seemed like very unrelated items to Charlotte.

"Oh," he said as if surprised that she did not immediately see the connection. "They were developed for rheumatic patients."

"Were they indeed?" This was the first time she had seen interest in things medicinal put on display rather than just being something he told her he possessed. It was reassuring to know that he had been honest with her and had not said such a thing just to sway her opinion of him.

He nodded. "Quite so, I assure you, and they are tasty. I procured a parcel of them to bring back with me before I left Bath." He said it as if it were an important secret that only he and she should know. That thought made her smile for it made her feel special in a strange and likely nonsensical fashion.

"How do you eat them? Grandfather likes them with his port."

"Your grandfather is wise, for I find them to be excellent alongside a fine glass of some sort of wine. However, my favourite way to eat them is with a touch of jam and a bit of cheese."

"Jam and cheese? I have had them with cheese but never jam."

"If you like fruit paired with cheese, I am confident you would like the combination, and, I should think," his brow furrowed as if contemplating an idea, "that it would be one way to have a bit of something sweet without overindulging." One eyebrow cocked as if interested in the concept. "I shall have to ask Mr. Norman his opinion on that."

"Mr. Norman is one to champion moderation." Charlotte had heard Mr. Norman instruct her grandfather on not eating too much of any one thing – a bit of salted meat, a few sweets on occasion, just enough fat to add flavour and moisture but not a spot more, and so on. For the most part, her grandfather was happy to oblige his physician without too much grumbling. However, limiting desserts was a point of contention for him. She would have to write to him and suggest Mr. Chapman's combination of cheese and jam on his Bath Olivers.

"He most certainly is. He is quite brilliant if you ask me. I can see him discovering many things over the years for he is not one to be limited to what has always been. He is a forward thinker. I am quite honored to be his future assistant."

Charlotte could not help but smile at the exuberance with which Mr. Chapman spoke about matters pertaining to medicine and Mr. Norman.

"You are fortunate to be joined to him not only in profession but as a brother."

His smile stayed in place as he nodded. "I only wish I could have been his brother sooner, for Belle's sake."

"Not your own?"

He shrugged. "Perhaps I wish it somewhat for myself, but my desires and interests are trivial items when compared with love, such as my sister has for Mr. Norman, do you not think?"

Charlotte nodded. "Have you always thought this way? That is, have you always thought of your sister's happiness before your own benefit?" She had not thought he ever put anyone's happiness before his own. Apparently, her thinking on that had been incorrect.

"When it came to Mr. Norman yes, though I was not at liberty to express such an opinion."

"Is that because of your father?"

He nodded. "I should have spoken for her before now."

And his smile was gone, and the sadness that had been in his eyes earlier had returned. Perhaps he was also not so lacking in depth as he had always appeared to her to be.

"I dare say you will be happy to be living close to her."

A partial smile returned. "I will."

Again, silence settled between them.

"Mr. Chapman," Louisa said with urgency, "is it true that you have ridden a pig?"

Mr. Chapman's eyes widened and then narrowed as he shot his friend a displeased look. "Did Mr. Green tell you that it was because of that pig that we became friends?"

"No!" Louisa cried. "Is it true then that you rode it?"

"It is."

"I told her that we met on the night you rode a pig," Mr. Green explained. "Your willingness to ride Sir Hamhocks was what proved to me that you were a friend worthy of having. That was my point to the story, but Miss Louisa could not believe you rode a pig."

"I did not ride him far," Mr. Chapman continued, "to be perfectly honest. Though it will not reflect well upon me, I had indulged in a few too many cups of beverage, and keeping my seat on a pig who bore no saddle was a bit much for my coordination. Suffice it to say I smelled very poorly and was forced to walk behind the other fellows on our way home since we were walking into the wind."

"Why would you ride a pig?" Louisa managed to get the words out between giggles.

Mr. Chapman shrugged but shared a speaking look with his friend. "The portly steed was there. The challenge was given, and one does not back out of a challenge."

"You never back out of a challenge?" Louisa fluttered her lashes and sighed as if such a fact were the most wonderful thing she had ever heard.

"Not unless fulfilling it holds more dire consequences than meeting the contest does," Mr. Chapman answered. "For instance, I would not walk along the peak of a roof while inebriated unless the life of someone I held dear depended upon it. However, for a half-crown, I might attempt to dance in such a state on a stone wall no higher than my waist."

Louisa's face registered her bewilderment at such an explanation. "Do gentlemen often challenge each other to such... unusual things?"

"Often," her father said.

Louisa's head snapped toward her father. "Truly?"

"It is shocking that so many of us survive to be fathers," he added. "It is, in part, a portion of what moulds a gentleman into who he will be. It is a silly way to learn risk and reward, and most of us realize that even before we stand in the quadrangle and sing songs when we are supposed to be in our rooms."

"You did not!" Louisa voiced what Charlotte was thinking.

"I was young and foolish once."

"But you are so..." Louisa seemed lost for the right word.

"Sensible," Charlotte supplied before her sister thought of a less tactful way of saying it.

"Even sensible gents have their moments of tomfoolery."

"That is absolutely shocking," Louisa said.

Their father laughed. "I assure you it is true. The fortunate fellows realize their folly and eventually leave it behind. Those who do not, however, often live life far less enjoyably."

"And so do their friends and family," Mr. Green muttered.

"Precisely," her father agreed. "They are also the ones who, unlike Mr. Chapman, accept a challenge simply to prove themselves better than anyone else."

Charlotte recognized the nod that her father gave to Mr. Chapman, and from the replying nod that he gave her father, she knew that he did, too. While the nod might have only been given to encourage him, to her, it also conveyed the assurance that her father had not said he liked Mr. Chapman merely out of deference to his daughter's predicament. It appeared that he truly thought there was some goodness in Mr. Chapman. If she could just find that goodness, perhaps her mind would become untangled, and she would be able to allow herself to like Mr. Chapman as she wished to do.

"I think our discussion must move to the dining room if we wish to eat before our food grows cold," her father said.

They all rose and began arranging themselves to go in for dinner.

While Mr. Green was depositing his empty wine glass on the table near Charlotte, he whispered, "Do not let him mislead you."

Charlotte turned startled eyes to him.

"Chapman is no fool. He is a good friend. The best a fellow could have." He turned from her quickly and offered his arm to her sister.

"You look perplexed," Mr. Chapman said as he held out his arm to receive her hand.

She shook her head. "I was simply pondering... things." Such as why Mr. Green had said what he did, and what the look he and Mr. Chapman had shared during the relation of the pig riding story had meant.

"Are you certain?"

She nodded and allowed him to lead her from the room behind her parents. Halfway to the dining room, she leaned toward him and asked, "Why did you ride that pig?"

"To complete a challenge," he replied uneasily.

"What would have happened if you had not completed it?"

He sighed and cast a look over his shoulder.

"Another would have been asked to do something far more humiliating."

"And you could not allow that?"

His head bobbed up and down in an almost imperceivable nod.

She smiled, and a lightness bubbled up within her. She had found it! The glimmer of goodness. "I hate to disappoint you, Mr. Chapman."

His brow was furrowed when he looked at her in question.

"You were wrong," she teased. Teased. She shook her head. Had she ever teased a gentleman about anything unless it was her father or some other relation? Not that she could remember.

"About what?"

"You are not the complete opposite of Mr. Green." She lowered her voice. "I believe you might be concealing a good man behind your charming façade."

His steps faltered.

"And I think if I asked Mr. Green, he would tell me I am correct." And with that, she removed her hand from his arm and allowed a footman to help her take her seat to enjoy a dinner she had earlier been dreading.

# Chapter 5

"Would you kindly pay attention?" Tom thwacked Miles's knee. "We cannot study outside if all you are going to do is sit, looking up into the sky and counting the clouds."

It had been two days since Charlotte had mentioned finding enjoyment in the garden because it was where she liked to think. So far, he had found being outside a much more refreshing place to attempt his studies. "I am not counting the clouds," he said, "though I must admit it would be a far superior activity to comprehending Greek."

"Our examination will not include how many clouds passing overhead bore the shape of a dragon."

Miles chuckled. "I have yet to see a dragon, but that one, just there, does resemble a rat."

"A rat?" Tom peered up into the sky. "I do not see it."

Miles scooted to sit next to instead of across from Tom.

"The long nose is here." He pointed to the narrow right-hand portion of a large cloud. "And if you follow it back, just here." His finger traced the part of the cloud that grew wider. "Those are his haunches."

"And where is his tail?"

"Why, wrapped around him, of course."

"Conveniently," Tom muttered.

"Or logically," Miles countered. "You will notice he is elongated yet crouched. Therefore, I posit that he is cautiously stretched forward and sniffing. Perhaps that cloud in front of him is a morsel of food, but the rat does not know if a maid with a broom is hiding nearby or if the cat, which he earlier saw go out for a roam, has come back."

Tom shook his head. "That would make a lovely children's tale, but it does nothing to explain what Homer means in this passage."

Miles sighed. He might have been watching the clouds, but that did not mean he had not been listening. Indeed, watching the clouds had helped him attend to what his friend was reading.

"Life changes," he said by way of beginning his explanation of the passage. "Things can be progressing splendidly, and then, along comes a cloud of despair – perhaps in the shape of a rat." He smirked at Tom, who rolled his eyes. "And when tragedy begins to rain down on the fellows, sitting on the lawn, they can only push themselves close to the tree and hope that it will help keep them somewhat dry until a new day which is free from clouds – rat-shaped or otherwise – dawns and the time of trial disappears, and a happier time takes its place."

He looked to his friend for his acceptance or rejection of his interpretation.

"Your answer is a mite unorthodox, but it seems you have the basics of this passage."

"Can we please do something other than study now?" Miles pulled his watch from his pocket. "We have been sitting here for two hours. Surely, you must be parched from so much lecturing, and my eyes grow tired from watching clouds and my ears, weary from listening." He began to rise. "You know, you should consider being a tutor. I think you would excel at it."

"My father expects me to take up the estate in my turn, and I do not think I will be going to him and saying 'Please, Father, I would much prefer repeating the same discourses over and over to young men, who only wish to be done with the lesson before it has begun, to stewarding the estate. Perhaps, you could give the estate to Emmeline.'"

"Emme would do a masterful job of seeing that the place did not fall into ruin." Miles had met Tom's much younger sister twice. Both times had included a speech on something or another that involved why something which Miles had said or done was not proper. Though Emmeline had only been thirteen the last time she had skewered him with her sharp tongue, it seemed to Miles that she was well on her way to being a capable termagant, for she had not based her thoughts on anything illogical as some young girls might.

"That she would," Tom agreed. "However, I do hope that she will one day be inserting herself into the estate affairs of her husband and leaving me be."

"That will only happen if there is a fellow who

wishes for, shall we say, an overly confident wife."
It was the softest way Miles knew how to broach
the subject of Emmeline Green's demanding ways.

"Heavens! I do hope she softens before she
makes her debut, or I might always have her looking over my shoulder and inspecting my work,"
Tom said with a laugh. "She is so much like our
father."

Mr. Green, the elder, was the sort of gentleman
who demanded that things be done just so.

"You are like him as well," Miles said.

"I do not see how."

"You like things to be orderly and to be done
as you wish them to be done. However, I will give
you that you are more lenient, for if you were not,
you would not have retained me as your friend for
so long as you have." Miles, to this point in their
friendship, had often ignored how his friend
wished for things to be done, choosing rather to
please himself. It was a fault he would have to
address while he was attending to the other necessary improvements in his character.

Tom chuckled. "No truer words have been spoken."

Tom's father had not given his hearty approval

of Tom's friendship with Miles. In fact, he had cautioned his son about the connection.

"Do you think your father would be happier with our friendship now if he knew I have been cast aside by my father?"

Tom grimaced. "It is likely. He never had anything good to say about Sir Allen."

"It seems there are few persons of sense who speak well of my father."

Miles sighed. He had never considered himself so lost to good sense as he had ever since his father demanded that he break off his attachment to Charlotte and if he did not, the repercussions would be felt most profoundly by the lady. He had truly not thought his father would follow through on such a threat. Miles was, after all, his father's favourite, or so he had thought.

However, he had come to realize that he had only been his father's second favourite since Sir Allen favoured himself above all others. The first whisper about Charlotte's having left in a great hurry, as if she had something to hide, had taken Miles utterly by surprise. It had also opened his eyes to just how little and mean his father could be.

"Although," Miles continued, "now that I have

considered it after recent events, those who do speak well of my father are also the sorts of people who gather and suffer fools to make themselves appear above their neighbours." He shook his head. "How blind can one man be?"

Tom's expression was sympathetic. "Are we going to find something to drink," he asked, "or are we going to stand here discussing how easily a son, who is eager to please, can be unaware of his father's failings?"

Truth be told, Miles would welcome the opportunity to push his failures to the side for a while over a glass of something. "Where shall we imbibe? At The Drunken Boar or in my rooms?"

"I am willing to brave the crowds if it means I do not have to teach you anything further for a solid hour at the least."

"I was hoping you would say that."

Miles picked up Tom's bundle of books from the ground where they were neatly stacked and tied with a long leather strap. He swung the strap over his shoulder. The books landed against his back with a thud.

"I believe being your porter is fair payment for

your tutelage," he explained to Tom, who looked ready to protest Miles's actions.

"My books are not going with us to the tavern."

"Then, allow me to run them back to my room."

"There is no need to run," Tom said, "and I can put them in my room."

"Do you not trust me?" Miles teased.

Tom shook his head. "That is not it. It just seems foolish to put them in your room when my room is just one door away."

"I do suppose you are correct."

The two walked together in silence, content to keep company with their own thoughts. It was one of the things Miles appreciated about Tom's friendship. There was no need to be constantly chattering or attempting to impress each other as there sometimes could be in lesser relationships. Tom was as dear as a brother to Miles. Indeed, he was more at ease with Tom than he had ever been with either of his brothers.

His eldest brother, Andrew, had been a mirror image of their father. That is, he was an reflection of their father if the mirror had a smokiness to it which gave a fitting likeness with a few small alterations to the reflection. Miles's eldest brother's small alteration, when compared to their father, was that Andrew was cunningly ruthless. His wit was far greater than Sir Allen's, and he used it to promote himself and his father at all costs.

To Andrew, nothing and no one came ahead of family name and position. He had been the first to tell Sir Allen about Belle's seeming attachment to a mere physician. He had also been the one to employ a man to keep watch over both his sisters and his mother to make sure that none of the Chapman ladies succumbed to the lure of romantic notions concerning Mr. Norman and Belle. It had even been he who had convinced their mother to share Belle's secrets with her husband. To be perfectly truthful, Miles had not shed very many tears over Andrew's untimely death in a carriage accident, and those tears which had been shed, had only been for his mother's grief, not his own.

Thankfully, or perhaps not, Sidney, the second eldest and now heir apparent, was not like their father at all. He was tender-hearted where Sir Allen was cold. While this had allowed Sidney to develop a closer relationship with his siblings than Andrew had ever cared to do, it did put him at the disadvantage of being more easily swayed by

Sir Allen and, when he was alive, Andrew. It also made Sidney a tad unpredictable, for one never knew if what Sidney said he would do was what he would do.

Miles allowed Tom to enter their accommodation block ahead of him. He pulled the books off his back and held them in his arms. The content of these tomes and those which resided in the library was confusing and difficult and required a great deal of effort to parse and learn properly. However, he had the advantage of a tutor to explain and expound on them. And while he knew that he must learn the lessons contained in these books to achieve his bachelor's, it all paled in consequence to what he now understood to be of greatest value and the one lesson he must not only learn but also master to have a happy life.

Charlotte had both delighted and terrified him when he had seen her two days ago. She claimed she saw evidence of a good man within him. A good man.

He handed the books he held to Tom once Tom's door was open. How did one become a good man when one had only ever been taught to follow the example of a man who was anything but good?

"You do not need to stand in the corridor."

Miles's thoughts focused on the friend, who was standing just inside his door.

"Right," he said. "My apologies. I was lost in thought."

"Ah, you are returned."

Miles turned to find his tutor, Mr. Eyers, had just gained the landing to the floor they were on.

"You were looking for me?" It seemed an odd thing for the man to be looking for Miles when school was not in session.

"Yes, I was. I have been here twice today already. I know it was foolish of me to expect you to be in your rooms when the weather begs to be enjoyed and while the term is not yet started. I, too, enjoy a bit of fun when there are no lectures to give." Tall, stocky Mr. Eyers seemed to fill the corridor both with his presence and the aroma of a lack of soap and an abundance of poorly crafted fragrance.

"We were taking advantage of the good weather, but I assure you we were not having fun. We were, in fact, studying," Miles said.

"Studying?" The man looked as if his eyes would pop out of his head and roll away from the surprise of hearing Miles had been studying. "Both Mr. Green and you?"

"Yes," Miles answered, quite enjoying how the man's mouth flapped open and closed as if wishing to speak but finding no words. "I intend to earn my degree as is right and proper."

"You do?"

Miles nodded. "I have found my motivation."

"Indeed?" Mr. Eyers' head tipped. "A pretty motivation, perchance?"

"Excessively." Was there another in all of England so pretty as Charlotte Wesley? To the eyes of another, there might be, but not to Miles. To him, Charlotte was the ideal to which all others should aspire.

"Miss Wesley?" Mr. Eyers asked.

Miles's brow furrowed. "Yes, but how do you know?"

The man fumbled with his pockets before withdrawing a letter bearing the remains of a familiar seal and hand.

"My father?"

"Yes, yes. I have had a very detailed letter from him just today, which is why I am here. It did not arrive alone. There was a parcel." He smiled at Miles as if that should explain everything.

Mr. Eyers was an intelligent fellow. He had to be to teach the things he taught, but at present, his intelligence seemed to be on holiday.

"And you needed to find me because..." Miles's voice lifted in question as he let the sentence fall away.

"Oh, right. How doltish of me to forget why I was here. I have your allowance." He held out a small purse. "It has been curtailed, and not by me." He began unfolding the letter.

"There is no need to read my father's words to me. I know that he is not pleased with me."

"That is an understatement if there ever was one! However, he is not being wholly unreasonable."

Miles was not so certain of that.

"In consequence of your refusal to part ways with your pretty motivation..."

Ah, there. Mr. Eyers' wit was returning.

"Come inside," Tom said from his doorway. "I am sure this information should not be shared in a corridor."

Miles had considered the same thing. However,

he had no desire to smell Mr. Eyers in his rooms long after the man had departed. He would have to thank Tom for the sacrifice later.

"In consequence of your refusal to part ways with your pretty motivation," Mr. Eyers repeated as he followed Miles into Tom's room, "your allowance has been halved, but I am to tell you that should you find you have lost your motivation, so to speak, the full allowance can be reinstated."

"Half is better than I imagined I would receive." He had thought that he might have to write to his aunt to request financial assistance.

"He has no wish for you to not look the part of his son, even if you have given up that position to chase after..." Mr. Eyer's voice trailed off as he grimaced at what he saw on the missive he held. "Miss Wesley," he completed.

Miles was certain his father had not deigned to refer to Miss Wesley by her proper name. It had likely been some repugnant description that had caused Mr. Eyers' grimace.

"Your tuition." Mr. Eyers stopped. "How do I put this delicately?"

"Has he paid it?" If he had not, Aunt Augusta

would be notified post haste. Miles knew that she would take her brother to task over such a thing.

"He has, as long as you remain in school."

"Why would I not remain?"

His tutor's smile was patronizing. "If things are kept quiet, I am certain it will not be an issue. We shall carry on as if your status has not changed."

"I am afraid I do not follow."

"Nor do I," Tom muttered.

"I understand you are to be a father."

Miles snatched his father's letter from his tutor's hands and scanned the contents.

"My child?" he cried. So, the rumors were to now threaten him as well.

"That is to be our secret –"

"There is no child."

Mr. Eyers' eyebrows rose. "That is fortunate."

"There could not be a child," Tom inserted.

"You mean?" Mr. Eyers looked from Tom to Miles and back.

"I mean Miss Wesley is still a maiden. Pure as the driven snow," Tom clarified as Miles read his father's letter.

"That is not what I have heard."

"What we hear and what is true are not always

the same, are they?" Miles growled. He flapped the letter at Tom. "He will pay the school more if they arrange for my degree without an examination. In fact, I could be free from studying altogether if I so desire." He shook his head. "He says he realizes that I am not so capable as some young men. He questions my abilities, Tom. He does not wish to be embarrassed by my failure. Do you see it?"

"Not yet. Give me a moment to read," Tom retorted.

He should have known his father would not go away quietly.

"Does he not see how this information could damage his precious reputation?"

"He does." Tom glanced up from the letter. "You stopped reading too soon, or you skimmed too much. *It is unfortunate that he* – meaning you – *takes so much after his mother. Of course, the difficulties in birth, I am certain, did nothing to gain him an advantage. Would that he had inherited the Chapman intelligence. But, alas, he has not. I have never said such to him, of course, for I would not wish to injure his pride. However, that is why I have never insisted upon his taking up a profession.*"

"The repulsive liar!" Miles shouted. "I will be

taking those exams, and I will excel at them." He snatched the letter back from Tom and crumbled it in his hand. "Thank you for delivering my allowance, Mr. Eyers. If you will excuse me, I have Euclid to examine." After a glass of port and a period of venting his spleen.

"My letter –"

"I think it is best if I keep this," Miles said. "We would neither wish for the knowledge of my lack of intelligence and supposed fatherhood to inadvertently fall into the wrong hands nor for you to be blamed for it."

"That is very wise thinking, Mr. Chapman." Mr. Eyers backed towards the door. "I wish you well with Euclid." And with that, he left.

# Chapter 6

A warm breeze, bearing the sweet fragrance of new blooms, fluttered the thin curtains that muted the brightness of the sun in the upstairs sitting room of the Wesleys' home. Charlotte closed her eyes and drew a deep breath. Was there anything better than the freshness that came with spring? Flowers were blooming. Trees were once again gloriously green. Lambs, chicks, foals, and calves added a new note to the noise from the pastures. Everything was alive and bright. Life in the spring felt hopeful, and that was an emotion which she needed to wrap in her embrace and cling to with all her strength.

There were rumors circulating about her. Her mother's good friend Mrs. Levy had heard them.

"For you, Miss Wesley."

Charlotte opened her eyes to see Mr. Hillier, the butler, standing before her and holding out a letter.

"Is it from Grandfather?" Louisa asked eagerly. Correspondence of any sort, especially that which was not delivered to their father, always piqued Louisa's curiosity.

Charlotte looked at the address. "It is not from Bath." It was from Oxford, but it did not look like any of her friends' handwriting, and whoever had written it had not included his or her name on the outside of the envelope. Charlotte turned the missive over and studied the seal.

"Where is it from?" Louisa joined her on the sofa near the window and propped her hands and chin on her sister's shoulder while Charlotte ran a finger over the seal which was embossed with a large C on a field of entwined vines.

Could the letter be from Mr. Chapman? She had never seen his penmanship before, but the C on the seal seemed to point to him as the writer. She flipped it back over to look at how neatly her name was written on the front with just enough flourishes to make it look regal. That did seem to be how Mr. Chapman would write.

"Where is it from?" Louisa repeated as she snatched the letter from her sister. "Oxford!" she cried. "I bet it is from Mr. Chapman." She clasped the folded and sealed paper to her breast and sighed. "I should like it very well if Mr. Green would write to me."

"My letter, if you please."

Louisa took a moment to admire the envelope before handing it back to her sister "What do you think he has to say? Perhaps it is a poem."

"I doubt it is a poem."

She certainly hoped it was not a poem, for Mr. Chapman did not seem the sort of gentleman who wrote poetry. It would be a dreadful thing indeed to have to pretend to him that his efforts were enchanting if they were not, as she suspected they would not be. She broke the seal.

"If you do not mind, Louisa, I would like to read this before you do. Not that I can promise I will share it with you until I have read it, of course." She made a shooing motion, indicating that her sister should move to the other end of the couch on which they sat.

Louisa liked to be included in everything that was happening, and she rarely waited to be invited to join in on anything she found intriguing or fun.

"Did Father give Mr. Chapman permission to write to you?" There was a hint of annoyance in her sister's tone as she flopped in the corner of the couch away from her sister.

"Not that I have been told." However, she and Mr. Chapman were nearly promised to each other, so the fact that he had written to her was not so bad as it would have been if he were merely a gentleman to whom she had spoken at a few soirees.

"Will you tell Father about the letter?"

"Why would I not?" Even if she wanted to keep such a thing a secret – which she did not – Louisa knew about the letter and Charlotte never knew when such a delicious morsel of information might pop out of her sister's mouth.

"It might have something terribly romantic in it that would be embarrassing to share."

While Charlotte was loath to admit it, her sister's fascination with all things romantic might just prove that, for some ladies, there actually was such a thing as reading too many novels. "Would you, kindly, allow me to read what is written in it before you make any further suppositions?"

"Is it from Mr. Chapman?"

Charlotte scanned down to the signature. "Yes."

"Could you read quickly?"

Charlotte sighed. "I will read as quickly as I am

able." She turned her eyes back to the letter. She hated to admit it to anyone, even herself, but she was excessively curious about what Mr. Chapman had to say, and she was feeling more than a little flutter of excitement over the fact that he had written to her at all.

*Miss Wesley,*

*I know that it is most improper to be writing to you when I have not gained permission to do so from either you or your father, and I would not condemn you for reading no further than here, though I would be sorely saddened to hear that you did not read my letter.*

"He has not been given permission to write to me," she said with a glance at her sister. "He admits it in his opening."

The information did little to quell her sister's interest. In fact, it brought an unrestrained look of excitement to Louisa's features.

*I have sent a second letter to your father informing him of my forward action in sending this to you, and I hope that he will not hold it against me and remove his tentative approval of my suit.*

"He has sent a letter to Father telling him about this letter." If the rumours Mrs. Levy had heard were to grow, there would be nothing tentative about Mr. Chapman's suit. It would then be best to accept his proposal outright without any period of waiting.

Louisa's enthusiasm faded somewhat. "That was very good of him, I suppose?"

"It was." And it raised him in Charlotte's eyes. He was attempting to be all that was proper. Of course, it was entirely possible that behind his façade of being a dandy, he had always been so. It would fit nicely with what she had learned about him three days ago when he had admitted to riding a pig just to spare a friend some humiliation. To be honest, she had been hanging all her hope on that one example of his goodness. For three days, she had not questioned herself about her admiration of him. Instead, she had indulged herself and allowed several daydreams about a happy future with him.

"I know you are not reading, for I can see that your eyes are not moving," Louisa scolded.

"It is my letter, and I will read it however I choose."

Her sister sighed and scowled. "I would think that a lady who is nearly betrothed to a gentleman would be more eager to read what he has written."

"I am only nearly betrothed to him because his

father started rumours about me, and my reputation is not what it should be." That thought still stung. How could someone declare another unworthy without even knowing the person whom he maligned beyond the fact that her ancestors had not been gentry?

"Did you pay attention to Mr. Chapman at all when we were at soirees?" Louisa's tone was condemning. "He has been in love with you since he first met you."

"He has not." He was infatuated but not in love. The two were very different. One was steady and true while the other was fleeting.

"He has, too. A gentleman would have to be utterly in love to keep returning to the lady who rarely gave him a smile and spoke no more than a word or two to him – and then, those words were only spoken when she was absolutely required to do so." Louisa nodded when Charlotte looked at her in surprise. "Yes, you were that horrid. Do you not remember me suggesting that you should be more welcoming of Mr. Chapman?"

"You tell me that about every gentleman who begs an introduction."

"Only because you can be rather dowdy and stern."

"I am not dowdy. I dress very well – just as well as you do."

Louisa shook her head. "I am not talking about your clothes, my dear sister. I am talking about your air."

"I am not dowdy," Charlotte muttered. She was circumspect and particular. Neither of which was a horrid thing to be. Added to that was the confusion of wishing to like Mr. Chapman because he was handsome and entertaining when she knew, as any sensible lady does, that she should admire him for something far less superficial. She had not known what to do with such feelings. She was not certain she knew what to do with them now. "Do you wish for me to read this or not?"

"I am not stopping you from doing so."

"Yes, you are."

Louisa pressed her lips together and fluttered her lashes.

"You were," Charlotte said as she turned her eyes back to Mr. Chapman's letter.

*It has come to my attention, at a very unfortunate time since I should have been listening to Mr. Green explain some geometric concept to me, that beyond knowing, from my observation of you, that you are kind and beautiful and all that is charming, I know very little else, and I am eager to learn what I can.*

*You are, my fair Miss Wesley, a far more delightful subject to study than anything taught at university or researched in a medical journal. But alas, my need to apply myself to my studies and the somewhat bothersome distance between your home and my accommodations makes courting you, as I would wish to do, nearly impossible.*

She smiled. Perhaps he was capable of writing poetry, for his ability to convey his sentiments was good and his style of writing was engaging.

"What did he say? Is it romantic?"

Charlotte's cheeks warmed. "A trifle. Now, let me continue reading."

*It is for these reasons that I am writing to both you and your father to request that we take up a correspondence about our days and our pasts. While I know that I have, to this point in my life, always been more than eager to talk about myself, I have never wished to share myself with anyone. (They are not the same things. I assure you.)*

*I have flaunted my abilities and entertained with sto-*

ries to gain attention for myself and my father, but I have never revealed my soul to anyone but Tom, my truest and dearest friend. Since I am determined that you and I shall one day be more dear to each other than any two mere friends could be, I would be honoured if you would allow me to tell you about my foibles and follies, as well as my hopes and fears, and I would be whatever word means beyond honoured to be trusted with knowing the intimate workings of your mind and heart.

I lay at your feet my complete and utter trust and devotion, and I await your reply.

Yours,

M. Chapman

If she were a less skeptical sort of person, she would have to say that Louisa was correct, and that Mr. Chapman was in love with her. But that made no sense. He admitted in his letter that he knew little about her. One could not fall in love with someone whom one only imagined but did not know. Still, the less practical part of her wanted to believe it and swoon dramatically against the back of the couch while she fanned herself with his words of "complete and utter trust and devotion."

"May I read it?" Louisa had scooted back to Charlotte's side.

Charlotte looked at the page she held. "I do not know." Did she want to share a letter that felt so private with her sister? Would doing so be offensive to Mr. Chapman?

"Is it terribly romantic?"

She nodded. "It really is." He wanted to know her. He wanted to share himself with her. He wanted to be dearer than any two mere friends could be. If he did not find success with Mr. Norman, helping him compile and publish his research, Mr. Chapman should consider taking up his pen to write on matters of the heart, for he seemed to have a flair for it.

"Please, may I read it?" Louisa begged. "I promise never to mention it to anyone but you."

Charlotte bit her lip as she considered sharing the letter. It would be nice to have someone in whom to confide. She and Louisa had often shared secrets when they were younger. It was only Louisa's tendency to forget that a secret was a secret that worried her.

"It is not an improper letter, is it?"

"No, not at all." While each sentence had conveyed a great amount of Mr. Chapman's desires, none of it had been presented inappropriately.

"How will I ever know what a proper romantic letter should be if I am not exposed to examples of such? Is that not why Miss Felding made us study some prescribed literature before she allowed us to choose our own books to read?"

Charlotte chuckled. "I am absolutely certain that reading Mr. Chapman's letter to me cannot be compared to examining examples of literary greatness."

"I think it can. Please, Charlotte, please?"

She looked again at the letter she held. Louisa did learn better when given examples to follow. "I cannot promise to let you read any other letter he sends me."

"Will you share bits of them with me?"

"I really do not know if I will be able to." She held Mr. Chapman's letter out to her sister. "You will understand why when you read this."

"Oh, it must be horridly romantic for your face has never been so red." She took the letter. "He writes very prettily – though I suppose I should say he has a handsome hand so as not to offend his gentlemanly sensibilities." She peeked up at Charlotte. "Do you love him?"

Charlotte shook her head. "Not yet." But there

was hope that one day, maybe even soon, she would.

# Chapter 7

"My apologies. If you could just step right." Miles squeezed between the wall and a large group of fellows at a table at *The Drunken Boar*.

Tom slid through the opening behind him. "Why must we always sit at this table? There was one in the other corner that would be far quieter."

"I like this table."

It was positioned just how Miles liked. He could see out the window without being right next to it, and he could also see the door. It was not where his father would have chosen to sit, for there were too many patrons to get in the way of being the first person to be seen upon arrival by anyone of note. But it did not matter what his father thought about anything anymore – well, except for that he thought his son was not intelligent enough to pass his exams and that he thought it acceptable to tarnish the name of a young lady simply because his none-too-intelligent son had fallen in love with her. Miles was once again reminded of the fact that his father only cared for one thing – himself – and Miles was determined to become his exact opposite.

He turned to Tom as a thought struck him. "If no one was in this establishment when we entered, where would you choose to sit?" He had never once thought to ask his companion's opinion on such a thing. He had always just insisted that his way was the only and the best way. How very Sir Allen of him.

Tom shrugged. "I suppose it would be wherever one of my friends was sitting."

"But what if your friend allowed you to choose?" Which, Miles realized, he should have done. "Or suppose you arrive before any of your friends? Where would you choose then?" As he asked the question, he determined in his mind to move to whichever table Tom named if it was unoccupied.

Tom stood, looked around the room, and shrugged. "I would probably choose to sit here. It would afford me the opportunity of hailing my friends upon arrival for, when there are not five men standing in the way, one can see the entrance quite well from here."

Miles smiled. "Then, are you saying that my opinion about where to sit is excellent?"

His companion closed his eyes and shook his head. "I do not want to, but yes. You have selected well."

"I thank you for your approval, and for accommodating my wishes. I know you do not like to press your way through a crowd."

He settled back and pulled out the missive he had just received before he and Tom had left their rooms. It had not been easy to wait until they reached the pub before reading it. However, Tom had prepared some questions for him to discuss, and Miles had not wanted to put him off. It was imperative that he learn all he could if he were to have a chance of proving his father wrong and, at the same time, gaining Mr. Wesley's consent.

Tom took up his mug of ale that had just been deposited on their table. "Has she agreed to write to you?"

Miles nodded.

"That is good news," Tom said and then fell silent so that Miles could read.

*Mr. Chapman,*

*My father has commissioned me to tell you of his approval of your letter writing scheme. He trusts you will be honorable in all your correspondence, and he has instructed me that if you are not, I am to give your letter to him, and he will call on you.*

Those were direct enough instructions, for there was no way they could be read as anything other than behave or be cut off.

*Of course, I would not accept a letter that was less than proper, and I do not fear you would attempt to send me such. I just wish for you to know that my father's position on this matter is no different than my own.*

He had known she would not accept an unscrupulous letter.

*Thank you, both for your letter and the means for becoming better acquainted. I hope you do not mind, but I shared your letter with Louisa. I have informed her that I cannot guarantee that she can see any other letters we share since private matters should be kept just that, private.*

She wished to know him better. That was a wonderful thought. Miles also found comfort in her promise of privacy for it demonstrated a level of respect.

*I am uncertain where to begin. I have never written to any gentleman other than my grandfather and father before. I suppose I will begin as I do for them.*

Being categorized as a relation was not so bad a thing – so long as it was not as a brother.

*I am well, as are my parents and sister. The weather, as you know, has been delightful. I have spent several days in the garden. One day, I sat while Louisa attempted to take my likeness. She is not, I fear, destined to be remembered to the world as a great artist, but her sketches are precious to me. Another day, I helped Mother arrange some plants that had been started in the conservatory. She is confident that the weather is warm enough for them to flourish. A third day, I indulged in reading while the sun warmed me. Do not tell my mother, but I did not keep my bonnet on the whole time. I removed it for the length of six pages.*

He chuckled. Six pages! How scandalous!

*I fear you will find my life to be quite a boring topic about which to read, but I will persist.*

Miles smiled and took a sip of his ale. There was little about her life that bored him. Indeed, hearing about the mundane tasks of life was somehow more intimate than any prose found in a bawdy basket. Not that he would ever admit to Charlotte or her father that he knew what sorts of obscene books could be found in a bawdy basket. It had been curiosity that had prompted him to purchase that one book, and he had never added anything further in that vein to his library.

*I have reached the halfway mark on a cross-stitch project that I am making to hang on the wall in my room. It is, as you may guess, a garden scene so that I can have a bit of colour to look upon even in the dark shadows of winter.*

Flowers. He must make a note of the fact that she loved flowers and plants. She might enjoy the botanical gardens. Perhaps if she came to town?

*It is not that I mind winter overly much. It is just that I prefer spring, which, I can hear my father say, would not be possible without enduring winter first. He does like to torment me at times with his logic, but then, he does not scold when I return it in kind.*

Ah, father and daughter were somewhat alike. This was good to know.

*I must go practice the piano, so I will write again later. I would save this piece of paper and add to it before sending it off to you. However, if you are as eager to know the answer to a question you propose as I am, then to make you wait would be unconscionable. I appear to be patient, and I assure you I have a great deal more of that virtue than does my sister, but I must admit it is still in scarcer supply than I would like.*

She played the piano. He knew that from a musicale he had attended. She did not like to waste things. That seemed to fit her personality, and it was an excellent quality to find in a wife, especially if one's inheritance was no longer one's inheritance. And she willingly admitted to being impatient, which meant she was not, in fact, perfect, though he still thought she was as close as any young lady might hope to be.

*I pray your studies are going well. Give my greetings to Mr. Green, and Louisa's as well (she insists that I include her). I will eagerly await your reply, for I am anxious to know in detail the sort of man you are.*

*Ever-*

*Miss C. Wesley*

A large smile spread across Miles's face.

"What did she say that has you looking so pleased with yourself?" Tom asked.

"She wishes to know about me."

"That is it? Her wanting to know about you is all you need to be so delighted?"

Miles folded the letter and tucked it carefully

into his pocket. "Yes. That is all I need for now. She told me about how she spent some of her days, which means she is willing to tell me about herself, and then, she said she was anxious to learn about me. You do know what that means, do you not?"

Tom shook his head. "My apologies, but you will have to explain that."

"It means she is not indifferent to me, and I have hope of succeeding if I stay my course."

"I had no doubt you would succeed," Tom replied.

"Yes, you did." He lifted his mug. "To success," he said before taking a large draught of his ale.

"To success," Tom repeated. However, his mug was empty, so the toast was not so effective as it could have been.

"I've not seen you in an age." William Clark, a short fellow with a round face and a perpetual smile, sat down at their table. "If I were taller, I might have seen you earlier. I've been over there." He tipped his head to the left. "Haworth has his dice, and he's been doing a mighty fine business with them."

"Have you figured out how he does it yet?" While Mr. Clark was short in stature, he was taller than Goliath when it came to deducing things and working mathematical problems.

Clark shook his head. "I'd need to feel his dice to see if one is heavier than another, but they do not roll as I would expect them to."

Haworth was not known for his upstanding moral character. He was a shuffler if there ever was one.

"I heard that your father and you are not on speaking terms," Clark continued.

"Where did you hear that?" Miles asked.

Clark's brow furrowed. "I couldn't rightly tell you who said it, but I heard it not more than an hour ago."

"While you were here?" Tom asked.

Clark nodded. "You know me, Chapman. I am no wag. I am simply curious to know if it is true."

"More or less," Miles answered cautiously.

"Because of that pretty Miss Wesley?" Clark smiled fondly. "I like her. She is just the right height and so kind."

The right height was any lady who was not taller than Clark. Charlotte and Mr. Clark were almost exactly the same height. Mr. Clark came out ahead on that comparison but only by an inch or so.

"He does not approve of our courtship," Miles answered.

Clark leaned in. "Now, remember, I am only mentioning this because I heard it, and I am not going to share it with anyone else." He looked left and right before continuing. "I heard you and she were doing more than courting, if you catch my meaning."

Miles expelled a breath as if he had been punched in the stomach.

"You'd not heard that either?" Clark asked.

Miles shook his head. He had heard the rumours about Miss Wesley rushing away to Bath because of a rendezvous with some gent who was never named, but other than having heard what his tutor said was in his father's letter, this was the first time he had heard his name paired with Charlotte's in such a way.

"Miss Wesley is all that is good," Miles said. "Those tales about her and me are manufactured. We are courting and hope to marry next year." At least, he hoped to. She was still determining her desires on that account.

"Are you betrothed?" Clark asked in surprise.

"Not officially. I still have my schooling to complete."

Clark leaned back in his chair, folded his arms across his chest, and smiled broadly. "You are one lucky gentleman if you are to marry her."

"Is Chapman marrying or is it Green?" Haworth had apparently run out of pockets to empty. He laughed. "Must be Chapman. Green is too studious to notice a lady long enough to consider marrying her."

"He is not," Miles retorted.

Haworth placed his hands on the table and leaned forward. The aroma of alcohol and tobacco rolled off him, leaving Miles to wonder if any of the money he had won in his unscrupulous games had made it to his pockets or if it had all been spent already.

"Heard you already played the part of husband to that Wesley chit," he said.

Miles's heart hammered against his chest. His hands clenched into balls beneath the table. How dare this oaf speak that way about Charlotte! "I am afraid you are mistaken. Miss Wesley is not the sort of lady to allow that."

He blew out a laughing breath. "I heard her

skirts are lighter than smiling Sally's." He glanced over his shoulder. "Sally," he called, "come kiss me."

The pleasingly plump barmaid leaned over the counter behind which she stood in such a way that any material which covered her breasts seemed to disappear and all that could be seen was billowing flesh. "Only a kiss?" She batted her lashes.

"For now," Haworth replied. "Four kisses – one for me and one for each of these chaps."

"How scandalous, Haworth." She moved from the bar to come to where he was. "Will you enjoy the spectacle?" She asked as she pressed herself against him and allowed a hand to run up his back before it draped over his shoulder.

"No, he will not," Tom said. "For he is the only one who wishes to kiss you."

Haworth guffawed. "See what I mean? He has no idea what to do with a woman." He clapped Sally on the derriere.

"Tom is right," Miles inserted. "None of us wish to kiss Sally." He shot a questioning look at Clark, who shook his head. "And it has nothing to do with whether or not we understand what to do, as you say, with a woman."

Haworth sneered. "We know you know what to do with one." He leaned toward Sally. "He got a chit with child. Sent her running to Bath, but everyone knows."

"She is not with child, nor could she be," Miles growled.

Haworth dug some coins out of his pocket and slapped them down on the table. "It's yours." He slid the money toward Miles. "My payment to you for fifteen minutes with Miss Wesley to prove which of us is correct about her maidenly state."

Miles leapt from his seat and his fist met with Haworth's nose. "You will not speak about her in such a way," he said as he hit Haworth again, causing him to stumble backward.

Tom grabbed his arm before he could punch the fellow again. "Run," he hissed.

Haworth was shaking his head to clear it.

"He will kill you. Run. He is too large and lumbering to catch us."

And Miles, knowing that his friend was the smarter of the two of them, did just that. He pushed his way out of the pub and, with Tom at his side, ran as if chased by the devil.

# Chapter 8

"What are you reading?" Mr. Wesley sat down next to his daughter on the edge of the fountain in the middle of the walled garden.

The sun was slowly climbing its way into the sky. Dew still clung to the plants in the beds that circled the fountain except for where they were interrupted by walkways.

Charlotte flipped her book open to the title page of the novel she was not presently reading but was, instead, using as a concealment device.

"I thought you had already finished this book?"

Charlotte could feel her cheeks warming under her father's skeptical look. "I did, but I wished to read it again. There are so many different details that stand out when one reads a book a second or third time."

"I will not deny that. In fact, I will say it is

because you already know the path the story will take, and because of that, you can pay attention to the scenery along the way instead of just attempting to find the destination. However, it appeared to me as if you were not actually reading about the Dashwoods."

She sighed and opened the book to where a letter was tucked between the pages. "It is silly," she said.

Her father took the book from her and examined the letter. "Why is reading Mr. Chapman's letter silly?"

"Because I have read it before." Many times, truth be told.

Her father shrugged and handed the book back to her. "Many people reread letters – just as they reread books." He winked at her. "It helps us keep the writer close to us even when he or she is far away. Do you like Mr. Chapman enough to wish he were here?"

She bit her lip and shook her head while keeping her eyes on her book. "It seems I do."

"Are you still questioning whether or not you should like him?"

"No, but should I be?" That was the doubt which

had plagued her recently. She had allowed herself to accept both that she longed for Mr. Chapman to admire her and that she admired him in return – even if her admiration was likely more closely related to infatuation than it was to love, she would not push it away. However, there was this part of her that worried about how easily she had given in to her desires. "Should it not take longer, and more than one pleasant dinner and a well-written letter, to decide to like someone?"

Her father chuckled. "It took one look at your mother for me."

"One look? How can that be? You cannot know anything about a person from a single look."

"The heart does not always make sense." He put an arm around her shoulders. "While I confess it was your mother's beauty which drew me to her at our first meeting, I soon discovered that it was not just her face and figure which were lovely. Her heart was kind, and her character was exemplary. It was as if my heart knew what I was looking for and led me to her, but then, we tend to find that for which we are looking, do we not?"

*Seek and ye shall find.* Her father loved to quote that scripture to her when she had a problem that needed an answer. It was one of his endearing and yet annoying habits. He'd present her with a truth and then leave her to wrestle with determining the solution to her problem until she either discovered it or admitted defeat and sought more counsel.

"Now, that is not to say," her father continued, "that one should blindly follow one's heart. The heart can be deceived. So, allow yourself to feel what is in your heart and test it. Weigh carefully what you know – all of it. Do not just take the bits and pieces you wish to be true. Look for the good, but assess its veracity."

"Is that why you gave Mr. Chapman a year to prove himself?" Was her father testing what his heart was telling him was true to see if it was, indeed, true?

Her father squeezed her close. "In part. I am quite certain that I can judge his character before a year has passed, but he needs the time to settle into his new life before he adds a wife to his responsibilities, although, he may prove to me that a year is not needed for that. Only time will tell. After all, he has already won you over – at least, in part."

Charlotte sat, safely embraced to her father's side, and pondered just how perplexing the realm of emotions and attachments could be. A lady was not to be led by her passions, but she was also not supposed to deny them completely. There was a tricky balance to discover and maintain. Neither the heart nor the head was to be an all-consuming master.

"Well," her father said after some minutes of quiet repose, "I am going in to have my coffee, but before I do, you may want this to add to your book." He withdrew a letter from his pocket.

"Is it from Mr. Chapman?" She knew the answer before her father confirmed that it was indeed from Mr. Chapman for, by reading his first letter so many times, she had come to recognize the style of his letter formations.

"It was included in a missive of thanks from him that I received yesterday. He is most pleased to be granted permission to correspond with you." He chuckled and shook his head. "He seems to be well-versed in etiquette, and I am more and more assured that his affection for you is not a passing fancy." He stood. "I did not open those few letters, which I received yesterday, until this morning, and I have not yet dealt with all of what is there. However, I knew when I saw that letter that you would wish to have it just as soon as possible."

"You knew that?" Her fingers fairly itched to open the missive and read it.

He nodded. "You have been reading that book for days and have yet to get any further than one-third of the way through it."

"Oh." How obvious of her not to shift the letter forward a few pages each day!

"I have not read your letter," he assured her. "I trust you will inform me of anything that requires my attention."

"Of course."

"Go on, then. I will leave you to it."

Charlotte waited only until her father had turned toward the house before she unfolded the letter she held.

*Miss Wesley,*

*I wish to thank you for your letter. I must say I was eager to open it as soon as I received it. However, Tom was just as eager to quiz me on several Greek texts, so I obliged him before I indulged my own desires. I am to pass on to you that he was happy to receive both your greeting and that of your sister. He sends his in return.*

*Do I rightly suspect a fondness for my friend on Miss*

*Louisa's part? I promise I shall not divulge the truth of the matter one way or the other, but, as you rightly guessed, I am a curious fellow and impatient to know the truth of the matter. All that I can draw out of Tom on the topic of your sister is that she seemed a pleasant sort of young lady and was most assuredly pretty. He has not admitted to anything more than that.*

It would be lovely if Mr. Green liked Louisa, for Mr. Green seemed a sensible sort of fellow, and Louisa was not the most sensible girl. Therefore, the combination of personalities would present a good possibility for a happy and unshifting life. However, Louisa was only seventeen, and she found many gentlemen to be worthy of sighing over. Be that as it may, Charlotte hoped that fortune would shine on them and that Mr. Green would rise above the rest.

*I am well – save for a few scrapes and bruises, most of which are from taking a fall two days ago. The rest are from a small joust with another fellow. None of it is worth an ounce of worry. I have sustained worse injuries in my life. For example, when I was five, I sprained my wrist when I fell while climbing over a stile, and when I was eight, I cut my thumb while trying to use a knife* to carve my name in a tree. That injury required three stitches.

*Do you know who kept me company and saw to my bandages and poultices while I was required to rest for several days to aid my healing? My sister, Belle. She is perfectly suited to be a physician's wife. She always has been. I think she has always been as interested in medicine as I have been. I also think you and she could be good friends. I hope that I will one day get to discover if my opinion is correct or not.*

Charlotte was confident his opinion was right, for the few times, during her stay in Bath, when she had spoken to his sister, Charlotte had found Mrs. Norman to be delightful.

*I find I have become somewhat nostalgic of late as I have pondered my life and upbringing. There were parts of it that were very good, but, having finally learned what I have regarding my father, even those happy portions have fallen victim to skepticism for I view my father's actions in a whole new light. I am resolved to be the sort of father who never causes his children to wonder about the motive for my actions toward them. They shall not have to wonder if the presents they receive were given out of love or to make me appear to be the sort of father all others should aspire to be. I fear that was the motiva-*

*tion behind many of my father's gifts. I would hope I was*
*wrong, but I cannot. Not now.*

Charlotte's hand rested on her heart. How
dreadful to be the child of such a parent. It must
be something which would be horrendously difficult to rise above, for she imagined there would be
lingering doubts. It would be her job, should she
marry him, to allay his fears and help him rightly
see his actions, would it not? Was that not what
one friend did for another, and was not friendship
part of marriage? It had always been so in her mind.
She had always planned on marrying a gentleman
with whom she could be a friend, as well as a lover,
mother of his children, and manager of his domes-
tic affairs. That was one reason why her attraction
to Mr. Chapman had caused her so much trepidation. There was no friendship between them. They
were barely acquaintances. The foundation of such
a relationship seemed, in her mind, to be destined
to crumble at the first onslaught of foul weather.

She stared at the path in front of her. Perhaps
she had been wrong in her assessment. Perhaps
attraction and friendship could happen in either
order. One could be friends who grew to love one
another deeply, or one could be attracted to some-

thing about another person, much like her father was attracted to her mother's beauty, and then, because of and through that attraction, a friendship birthed alongside lasting love could develop. That must be it. Satisfied with her reasoning, she turned her eyes back to the page she held.

*I have likely shared enough of myself for one letter. I would hate for you to think that I am a maudlin sap. I do not believe I am, though I find I may be given to being such at times. It likely reflects poorly on me to admit that fault, but I would have you know the sort of man you are considering.*

How was it being a maudlin sap to think seriously about what one had endured and how one wished to be? Was it because he was sharing such intimate things with her? It was as it should be. In her opinion, which she hoped was not too revolutionary, but feared it might be, there was absolutely nothing wrong with revealing such private thoughts. Indeed, it recommended Mr. Chapman very highly to her. She had heard Mrs. Levy moan about how Mr. Levy rarely told her what he was thinking until he had come to a conclusion. He was a wonderful man, Mrs. Levy would say, but she longed to know what went on in his mind more often than she did. She was right. Mr. Levy was a wonderful and sensible gentleman. However, he was most decidedly on the reserved side.

*I also do not wish to spend all my time talking about myself. I have done so for most of my life, and I am making every effort to no longer be as I have been, and truly, I wish to hear more about you than I wish to speak about myself. Please do not be too long in replying, and please, ask me what you will. For, I shall not feel as if I am speaking of myself unnecessarily if I am answering your questions.*

*Before I conclude, I shall do what I am requesting of you to do. I would dearly love to hear about your childhood. I imagine it was very happy because I cannot think that anyone would be unhappy with a father like yours. Did you have any favourite games or treats? (I had a favourite wooden horse that I took with me everywhere that my father would allow until I was seven.) Which parts of your childhood do you hope to bring forward to your own family in the future? Are there any parts which you would lay aside?*

*I will be eagerly awaiting your letter.*

*Yours,*

*M. Chapman*

"Ah, there you are!" Louisa cried from the gate

to the walled garden. "I thought you would be eating breakfast by now."

"I am on my way to do that now." Charlotte folded the letter she held and tucked it inside her book.

"Was that a letter from Mr. Chapman?" Louisa asked eagerly.

"Indeed, it was, but I cannot share it with you. I am, however, supposed to let you know that Mr. Green was happy to receive your greetings and sends his in return."

"Does he? Did Mr. Chapman say anything else about Mr. Green?"

Charlotte shook her head, causing her sister to look somewhat disappointed.

"Maybe he did in this letter," Louisa handed an envelope to her sister. "Father sent me to find you and deliver it."

"This does not appear to be Mr. Chapman's writing." Charlotte broke the seal and unfolded the sheet of paper. Her eyes scanned to the bottom. "It is from Mr. Green," she said as she lifted startled eyes to Louisa.

"Mr. Green? Whyever would he write to you?"

"*Miss Chapman*," Charlotte read aloud, "*I know*

*this letter should go to your father, but my friend insists that it be sent to you. I am afraid to unsettle Miles any further than necessary, so please see that your father and mother are made aware of the fact that we will not be able to attend the dinner planned for Saturday. We thank them for the invitation, which we just received this morning."*

"Not attend dinner?" Louisa cried. "But they must!"

That was precisely how Charlotte felt about the news, but rather than indulge her disappointment, she continued reading.

*"Miles told me that he had mentioned to you that he had fallen and received some cuts and bruises – though not all were from the fall. He insists I be clear on that. He is honest to a fault with his friends, even when it does him a disservice, but that is not my purpose in writing. I just wished for you to know that about him.*

*"One of his scrapes has caused a fever, it seems. Sweating, pain, and shivering only set in this morning, and I am currently waiting on the apothecary to arrive. Miles is telling me that I am to assure you that he will soon be well and not to worry. My apologies for not being able to write to you with better news. T. Green."*

"Surely, his fever will be gone before Saturday," Louisa protested. "It is four days away."

Charlotte hoped it would be gone by then. "Do you suppose it is worse than Mr. Green is willing to say?"

Louisa's eyes grew wide. "Oh, I hope not! Do you think it contagious? Will Mr. Green become ill, too?"

"I doubt it very much," she assured her sister while her own mind raced with dire outcomes. "Come, Louisa. We must go share the news with Father and Mother." And perhaps convince her father or mother to take her to town to discover the extent of Mr. Chapman's illness for herself.

# Chapter 9

Miles opened his eyes just enough to see the shadow of someone entering his room. He thought to call out and check to see if it was Tom, but he was far too tired to form words and force them from his lips. Sleep. Sleep was all he wanted. At least, he was no longer shivering, and his nightshirt felt as if it was dry. He tried to open his eyes further but all that lifted were his eyebrows.

"He is in quite the state, is he not?"

What was his tutor doing in his room? Where was Tom?

"It is not the first time I have seen a pupil fall victim to the ravages of a dissipated life."

"Mr. Chapman is not sleeping off too much alcohol."

Ah, Tom was here. Miles once again attempted

to crack his eyes open – this time successfully. "Water," he managed to say.

"He has been ill," Tom continued, though Miles heard water pouring from a pitcher. "It is on the table next to your bed. Can you sit up and drink it?"

Tom was not the best nursemaid. He preferred not to touch a fellow who was ill. Of course, Miles could not fault him for that. Not everyone was comfortable in the sick room.

Miles finally managed to open his eyes and began to push up in his bed. Tom reached for his pillows and propped them behind him.

"Mr. Eyers wishes to speak with you," he whispered. "I tried to explain you were not fit for company, but he would not be put off."

"This is a matter of great importance." Mr. Eyers leaned over Tom who was finishing the fluffing of the pillows. "He does not smell of alcohol."

"That is because I have not had any in – how many days, Tom?" He had lost track of days after the apothecary had come and treated his wounds.

"Three."

Mr. Eyers stepped back to give Tom room to move away from the bed.

"Your eye does not look good," Mr. Eyers said.

"I do not recommend falling and scraping your face – or any other part of yourself, for that matter – on the road." Miles winced as he reached for the glass of water. He had fallen on his right side and scraped not just his face but also his arm, his side, and his leg in the process, although his face had gotten the worst of it since it had not been protected by cloth as the rest of him had been.

"And your hand? Is it that greyish-yellow on your knuckles from your fall, or was that from the brawl in the pub?"

Miles took a deliberately slow sip of water. Who had told Mr. Eyers about the incident at *The Drunken Boar?*

"From the pub," he replied, "but it was not a brawl. Two well-placed punches is all it was."

Without being invited to or asking if he could, Mr. Eyers took a seat in the chair next to Miles's bed, causing Tom to scowl and relegating him to sitting on the edge of the bed.

"And this was over that pretty motivation of yours, was it not?"

"I do not think I need to explain myself to you," Miles retorted.

"Your father would disagree." The man pulled an envelope from his pocket. "He was not pleased to hear about the altercation."

Whatever tiredness Miles might have been feeling moments ago flew away and was replaced with equal measures of wariness and fury.

"Did you write to him about it?"

"It is my duty to inform your father about any failings, whether they be in intellect or character."

"Failings in character?" Miles cried.

"Please," Tom inserted, "his fever has not been gone half a day. Must this be discussed now?"

"I am afraid it must." Mr. Eyers wore the expression he always wore when he was about to deliver a lecture that he deemed of great importance. "I have it on good authority that your inappropriate behaviour was not confined to the pub."

"How so?" Miles asked cautiously. Something foul was afoot. He could feel it from the prickling on the back of his neck to the dread in his belly.

"My room was entered forcibly."

"And you think I had something to do with that?"

Mr. Eyers nodded. "Someone saw you coming out of it."

"Someone? Does this someone have a name?"

"Not that I can give you," Mr. Eyers replied. "Your allowance was taken, along with a good, and rather expensive, bottle of wine."

Miles allowed the information to settle into his mind before asking, "Are you accusing me of stealing my own money?"

Mr. Eyers nodded. "And a bottle of wine."

"Which my father, no doubt, sent you." Sir Allen was known to send gifts of wine to those he wished to keep in his favour.

"You have been cut off," Mr. Eyers said.

"No, he has had his funds decreased," Tom corrected before Miles could say a word.

Mr. Eyers unfolded the letter he held. "The person who saw Mr. Chapman exiting my room said he was not alone." He gave Tom a brief but pointed look.

"Now, wait just a moment!" Miles said. "Tom is as honest and noble as they come."

"Aye, he was, but he has been keeping company with you."

"I am not a degenerate. I have always abided by the rules, mostly."

"Mostly," Mr. Eyers repeated. Then, he passed

the letter he held to Miles. "I have not informed your father about the missing allowance and wine. At least, I have not yet."

The way his tutor added that last bit increased Miles's trepidation about what the letter he held might hold. Quickly, he skimmed the contents of the letter and blew out a breath before reading it more carefully. It seemed that he was about to be cut off completely. Sir Allen would not tolerate any relation of his behaving so poorly as to cause a scuffle in public. Should there be any further black marks placed next to the Chapman name, all funding would cease, for Sir Allen could not be condemned for breaking from a miscreant. And knowing his father as he now did, Miles was certain the break would not be done quietly. Sir Allen must, of course, be thought of as the victim so that his image would not be marred.

"Your allowance for next month has been sent to your aunt in Bath. You must see her to claim it," Mr. Eyers said.

"He must go to Bath to get his allowance? That seems rather preposterous," Tom said.

Miles shook his head with his eyes closed. His father was a scheming man! He would stop at nothing to get what he wanted. "He wishes for me to move to Bath so that he can be free and clear of me."

"No, no," his tutor corrected, "it is so you will be removed from the influence that has caused you to go against your father and has been the impetus of your downfall into ruinous acts."

"Precisely. He wishes to be done with me, and he wishes to be done in such a fashion as to have caused as much injury as he can."

"I cannot believe any father could be so cruel," Mr. Eyers cajoled. "Sir Allen simply worries for your future, and a dissipated life does not promise a bright future."

"Miles is far from living a dissipated life!"

"He is on the doorstep. Things must be dealt with harshly now to prevent any further slide into disgrace," Mr. Eyers explained.

Miles simply shook his head again. His father must be paying Mr. Eyers a pretty sum to have convinced a man who could read, write, and converse in Latin and Greek that Miles was one step away from plunging into the fiery arms of hell.

"If Mr. Chapman agrees to leave Oxford without incident, then I will have no need to write to either his father or yours, Mr. Green, about your breaking into my room, nor will I inform the magistrate of your actions."

Tom's mouth hung open.

"I will go," Miles said. That was the only solution that would save his friend from having his name blackened. "Amicably. Which means nothing further shall be said to sully my name or that of my friends, both Mr. Green and Miss Wesley."

"But –" Tom began to protest but fell silent when Miles shook his head.

"I can be gone in a day, provided my fever does not return."

"A day!" Tom cried.

Miles nodded.

"You should not be going at all," Tom protested.

"I must." The more quickly he complied with his father's edict, the safer Tom and Charlotte would be. He could not risk putting up a protest, for Sir Allen's next play might be truly damning. Mr. Eyers had already threatened to go to the magistrate.

Mr. Eyers pushed up from his chair. The man looked excessively satisfied with himself, and Miles wondered what his father would send to Mr. Eyers for having rid him of his problematic son.

He was not given to weeping. However, at present, Miles wished he was, for he felt the full sting of his father's actions and words as they sliced at him like a cat-of-nine-tails – each barb, each plot, was a blow that cut at his soul, wounding and only promising to stop tearing at him if he bent to the will of his tormentor. A tormentor who was supposed to have been a protector. He scrubbed his face and flopped back against his pillows as Mr. Eyers left the room.

"I will need for someone to carry a letter to Miss Wesley for me." He closed his eyes and blew out a breath. "And Mr. Wesley." They would likely be the last letters he would write to the Wesleys. There was no way he could complete Mr. Wesley's challenge now that he was being sent away from school.

"What will you tell them?"

Miles shook his head and shrugged. "Only that I have been removed from school and am going to Bath. That is the truth."

"It is only a portion of the truth," Tom said.

"It is enough. The less they know, the less

chance there is of my father doing them harm." Miles draped an arm across his eyes and wished that the circumstances which swirled around him could be blocked out as easily as the light from the window could be. "It was Haworth. It had to have been."

"I know."

The lummox had caught them after Miles had fallen. However, he had been too winded to do much more than shout some threats while Miles scrambled from the ground and found his footing enough to continue his flight.

"I did not think he was smart enough to construct a ruse such as our breaking into Mr. Eyers' room."

Tom chuckled bitterly. "Haworth's pockets are lined with his winning from playing unfair games and tricking those who have imbibed too much alcohol into believing they have a chance to win. He looks like an ox, but his mind is as sly as a fox's."

It was true. The man was known for fleecing his opponents in any game of chance they chose.

"I wish I had his cunning," Miles admitted.

"Why?"

"For then, I could conjure a means of besting my father at his own game." This feeling of being the hopeless prey of another was not one which Miles enjoyed.

"Look at me." Tom pulled Miles's arm away from his face. "You have already bested him. When you chased after Miss Wesley and sought out your sister to lend your aid in seeing her happy, you bested him."

"But I have lost Miss Wesley."

"No." Tom's voice was firm. "You will not lose her. I will not allow it."

"I cannot prove myself to Mr. Wesley if I do not complete my schooling, and why would Charlotte wish to join herself with a man who was asked to leave school? Even if she did, would she and I ever be free of my father?"

Tom sank down on the bed again, looking as grieved as one might expect to see from a man who had lost a large portion of what was important to him in the world. "It is not impossible." His words were positive, but his expression was questioning. A deep furrow formed between his eyes, and he tapped his lip as he thought. Finally, he smiled. A solution must have been found. "Be the opposite of anything your father could ever say you were. Gain allies and friends who would support you as I do."

Miles's lips tipped upward at that. Tom was the most steadfast friend a fellow could have. To gain even one more friend of such quality would be a feat worth attempting.

"And," Tom added, his smile broadening, "pass your exams."

"How can I?"

"I will write to you, and I am certain Mr. Norman would be of some help. You said he is brilliant."

"But I am not a student after today."

"If Mr. Eyers and the others here do not allow you to stand for your exam, stand in Mr. Wesley's study and give your recitation."

"What good will that do? I will not receive a degree."

"You will earn something far greater," Tom urged. "You will prove to your father that you are not intellectually inept, and you will prove to Mr. Wesley that you are resolute and of great character."

Miles's brow furrowed as he pondered the idea. It could work. Charlotte might not be completely lost to him. Slowly, he began to nod his head. "I will. I will continue my studies, but you must promise to write to me faithfully about everything you are learning."

"I will," Tom promised without hesitation.

"And you must also promise me one more thing."

"Anything."

"You must promise me that you will protect my Charlotte and her family with your silence. Mr. Eyers found out about the incident in the bar. And while I believe it was likely Haworth sharing the details with him, we cannot know for certain. My father must believe he has won. That is how Haworth does it. He lets his victim think he has a chance to victorious and then, he strikes."

"But they should know the truth."

Miles shook his head. "Not now. I will tell them, but not now. Promise me you will protect the Wesleys by keeping silent."

Tom's jaw clenched as he stared at Miles for a long, silent minute. Then, he sighed and pledged his oath to his friend.

# Chapter 10

Charlotte looked from the missive she held to the gentleman who had delivered it to her and back again. The words had not changed. It still read "*I have left school. Any correspondence, should you wish to send any, can be directed to my aunt's home in Bath.*" Below that were Mr. Chapman's signature and the directions to his aunt's house.

She sank down onto the couch next to her sister in Mrs. Levy's sitting room. "I do not understand." Tears felt perilously close. How could Mr. Chapman leave with so little to say in his farewell? His other letters had seemed so promising. He had seemed so earnest in his admiration. Was it all a game? Surely, she could not have been so mistaken in his character, could she have been? He loved her, did he not?

"He felt unable to explain further. I am certain

he will write once he has arrived in Bath," Mr. Green assured her. He had taken the seat next to the couch on which she and Louisa sat and was leaning forward towards her. "He was reluctant to go."

He smiled a sad smile and nodded when she looked at him as if he were trying to answer the questions she had been thinking. She would grasp onto that and hold to the idea that Mr. Chapman still loved her and was not fickle in his affections.

"But he was ill." It made no sense for a gentleman, who had just had a fever, to suddenly go on a trip. "Did he think he needed to see Mr. Norman?"

Mr. Green shook his head. "He has left school."

His expression seemed to be attempting to say something his words were not, but Charlotte could not decipher it.

"And he is not coming back?" Louisa asked.

Mr. Green's eyes shifted from Charlotte to her sister. "No."

"Why?" Louisa asked. "Does he not love my sister?"

"No, it is not that!" He looked back to Charlotte. "He loves you. It is –" He clamped his lips closed and grimaced. Whatever he was not saying was taking some effort not to say.

"What is it then?" Mr. Wesley asked. "He agreed to complete his schooling in order to claim Charlotte's hand – if she wished to give it to him, that is."

If? The way Charlotte's heart was breaking at the thought of Mr. Chapman deserting her truly made it impossible for her to question her feelings for the gentleman any longer. Her thoughts were well-sorted on that front. He was her happy future. No matter what his profession might be or if he ever earned a degree.

"I cannot believe he would leave school if he loved her," her father continued in the same nearly angry tone he had begun with. "I had thought his affection for her was stronger than this." He waved the letter he held. "I thought he would, at the very least, attempt to bargain with me to change my demands of him. Instead, I get an 'I can understand if you do not wish for me to converse further with your daughter and if you must withdraw your tentative consent'?"

"Why is he giving her up?" Louisa inserted.

Mr. Green blew out a breath. "I wish I could say, but I cannot."

"Cannot or will not?" Louisa crossed her arms petulantly.

"Both." Mr. Green closed his eyes and his face flinched as if admitting such were sharply painful.

Charlotte looked at her letter once again before taking the letter her father handed her and reading it. If he loved her as Mr. Green claimed he did, there must be a reason for his short farewells.

"Does he wish for it to look as if he is giving me up?" That was the only thing that made sense to her. She could not believe he was so capricious as to throw off his family and devote himself to studying and improving himself just to decide upon a whim that he had made an error. She certainly hoped he did not think of his admiration of her as an error.

"Is that what it is, Mr. Green?" she pressed.

Again, he grimaced. "I wish I could say, but I promised I would not."

Charlotte smiled and nearly laughed in relief. She was right. Mr. Chapman was not giving her up because he wished to do so.

"Can you tell me nothing?" she asked.

Mr. Green shook his head. "A vow is a vow, Miss Wesley."

"A clue!" Louisa cried as if they had just begun the most delightful game she had ever played. "Give her a clue. Lottie is terribly good at reasoning things out, and a clue is not the same as telling."

"Perhaps we should have some tea," Mrs. Levy interrupted. "I will not hear of Mr. Green leaving my home without having received all the kindness that is due him, and a cup of tea always helps things look brighter."

"A delightful idea," Mrs. Wesley agreed. "It is just what I would have done if we were at my house."

"Has Mr. Chapman departed already?" Mr. Wesley asked as their hostess left the room to arrange for refreshments.

"He has. About an hour ago. Just before your message asking about visiting him arrived."

Charlotte, Louisa, and their mother had travelled to Oxford today to spend the day with Mrs. Levy while Mr. Wesley called on Mr. Chapman to inquire about his condition. The plan had been that they would dine with the Levys tonight and sleep here before returning home tomorrow. A hasty note to inquire about such an imposition had been sent off just as soon as could be arranged after Mr. Green's letter about Mr. Chapman's fever had arrived the day before last.

"Was he truly well enough to travel?" Charlotte asked.

Mr. Green scowled. "I did not think so, but he would not listen to me."

"He was in such a hurry to leave then?" If only she could figure out what had him running away.

Mr. Green nodded.

"It is best to do what one does not wish to do as quickly as is possible, is it not?" Charlotte watched Mr. Green's expression carefully for any hint of an unspoken answer.

Mr. Green's brow furrowed. "I am not entirely certain I should answer that."

"I only wish to hear again that he did not want to leave me," Charlotte admitted softly. Louisa took her hand and squeezed it.

"I am certain he did not," her sister assured her.

"Miss Louisa is correct," Mr. Green said. "You were a great part of his reluctance in departing school. You were also the best part of his haste in leaving. I wish I could say more." He rose and paced to the window where he stood looking out at the street.

"I wish you could, too," Charlotte admitted. "I am happy to know he did not wish to leave me, but am I to understand that his leaving is on account of me? Is that why I inspired his haste in leaving while he was still ill?"

"I should likely not answer that, but it is not solely on your account. He has my interest in mind as well." He scrubbed his face.

Mr. Green and Mr. Chapman were such good friends! If Mr. Green were partly the reason for Mr. Chapman's departure, it was not the first time he had put himself out in service to his friend. That was it! Charlotte peeked at her companions. Mrs. Levy had not yet returned. "Does he have your wellbeing in mind like he did when he rode the pig?" she whispered.

Mr. Green turned towards her. "He told you that he rode the pig to protect me?"

She nodded.

He chuckled and shook his head. "Well, then, Miss Wesley, I believe you have provided me with the best clue I can give you about Mr. Chapman's hasty flight to Bath: sometimes you just have to ride the pig." He smiled as if a weight of a hundred pounds had been lifted from his shoulders. "I believe that says what I wish without breaking my promise too much. After all, he never told me that you knew why he rode the animal." His expression grew serious. "But you must not act as if you know he has not abandoned you."

Charlotte's brow furrowed. "Why?"

"Because doing so will cause him to fall off the pig."

"Is Mr. Chapman truly riding a pig to Bath?" Louisa asked in astonishment.

"No, my dear," her father answered. "Mr. Green is speaking metaphorically."

Louisa's nose wrinkled. "I much prefer it when people say what they mean."

"So do I," Mr. Green assured her.

"What happens if Mr. Chapman falls off the pig?" Louisa asked.

Mr. Green shook his head. "We do not know, but we suspect it will not be pleasant. Falls never are."

"It is his father's doing," Charlotte said. The pieces were falling into place.

"How do you reckon?" Mr. Green asked cautiously.

"Sir Allen has already attempted to harm my reputation because he does not approve of me. He has also disowned his son for not giving me up. Who else would care so much if Mr. Chapman has or has not deserted me? The rumour mill would find it a delightful tale to add to the others about me, but they would not be able to harm Mr. Chapman or you. It would only be me who would suffer. Therefore, unless Mr. Chapman has any other enemies, it must be his father."

Louisa clapped her hands. "I told you Lottie was exceptional at deciphering clues."

"Indeed, she is." Mr. Green retook his seat just as Mrs. Levy returned to the room.

"Has it all been sorted?" she asked with interest.

"No," Mrs. Wesley replied. "However, Charlotte has worked out that Mr. Chapman has left to protect himself, Mr. Green, and Charlotte from whatever scheme his father has in play."

"Such a father!" Mrs. Levy cried. "Pardon me, Mr. Wesley and Mr. Green, but I swear I cannot determine how a man's mind works so that he can treat his own child with such malicious contempt."

"Most men are not the sort who can do so," Mr. Wesley said. "However, I agree with your sentiment. It is unfathomable that a gentleman would be so enraptured with his own standing and appearance in society that he would threaten his son with harm." He held up a hand. "I know he is not the only gentleman to behave so badly. History is riddled with them, but one must not cast out the whole lot of us based on the deeds of a few."

"Oh, yes," Mrs. Levy agreed with alacrity. "I would not decry all gentlemen just because some are despicable, for I would not wish to be judged by the least of my sex merely because I am a woman. Just think what Queen Mary did right here in our own town! No, I would not wish to be judged to be like her. I would not."

Charlotte smiled at Mrs. Levy's vehemence. The lady was devoutly Anglican. Queen Mary was quite the opposite.

"Someone should call him out!" Louisa cried. "Or take up arms against him, like Queen Boudica, to avenge my sister."

"Dueling is illegal, and leading a bloody revolt against a baronet simply because he is too full of himself is a bit much," her mother answered. "But

I dare say I am not opposed to the feeling behind your desire, my dear."

"Nor am I," Mrs. Levy said.

"I should not say it," Mr. Green inserted, "but for the cause of preventing a tragedy, I will. There is a plan in place to see the evil overlord," he smiled at Louisa as he said those words, "defeated or, at the least, wounded. It will take patience and time, however, and I cannot tell you more than that."

"While I like the sound of that, Mr. Green," Louisa replied, "I am not sure I have a great enough supply of either patience or time to be satisfied with it."

"You will need to find some," her father said, "for I am not in the habit of allowing my daughters to engage in battle with anyone."

Louisa sighed, and a scowl settled on her expression. She was not the sort of girl to disappoint her father, no matter how much she might wish to do so. She spoke of rebellion on occasion when she came up against a rule she did not like, but rebellion was not in her blood. It was also not a part of Charlotte's make up, but, at present, if she could think of a way to send Sir Allen reeling backward, she would do it. If Mr. Chapman could be brave and face dire consequences on her behalf, surely, she could repay him in kind, could she not?

Her father stood. "I am going to ride home and then towards Bath."

"What? And not have tea?" Mrs. Levy asked.

"If you would be so kind as to have a flask made ready and a lunch wrapped for travel," he replied. "Do you know which route Mr. Chapman took?" he asked Mr. Green, who thought he did. "Well, then, that is the direction I will go." He kissed the top of Louisa's head and then Charlotte's before holding her face between his hands and assuring her that he would be certain her young man had arrived safely at his aunt's house.

"May I?" he pointed to the letter Charlotte had received from Mr. Chapman. "I will see that the directions are left on my desk for when you return home."

"You will send word as soon as you reach Bath and see that he is well?"

"Of course," her father replied before turning to her mother and extending a hand. "Walk with me, my dear."

"Will Father going after him make him fall off the pig?" Louisa whispered to Mr. Green.

"No," he answered. "It seems the sort of thing a father might do if a gentleman abandoned his daughter. I wish I had thought of that, for if I had, I would have felt much easier about Mr. Chapman's departure today."

"I do hope nothing dire has befallen him," Louisa said.

"He is too clever for that," Mr. Green assured her as he held Charlotte's gaze with an intensity that begged her to know he spoke the truth.

# Chapter 11

A rut in the road scolded Miles loudly for travelling while not quite well. His body ached when staying still. Being jostled about only increased his discomfort. He could have, and likely should have, waited one more day before departing for Bath. However, leaving today had been hard enough, and giving himself another day to think about what he was giving up before actually giving it up would neither have made his departure easier nor strengthened his resolve to do what must be done.

He slowed his horse as he drove past the entrance to the drive that led to the Wesleys' home. This side journey would make his trip to Bath longer, but he simply could not drive past the road that led here without turning.

He could see no one at the front of the house except a servant doing something. Was he sweeping a step? Polishing a knocker? Shaking out a rug? It really did not matter, for it was not of any true interest to Miles. His interest lay with one particular young woman of the house, not with any of the servants. He had been hoping to catch a glimpse of Charlotte outside or at a window. He wished for just one more look at her. Well, actually, he longed for a lot more than a passing peek. He wanted to spend a full day with her, followed by another day and then, another and another, until all the days he had been allotted in this world were gone and his body was laid in the ground.

A short distance beyond the driveway, he drew his carriage to the side of the road and stopped. Charlotte was fond of spending time in the garden. However, he knew there was no way he was going to get a glimpse inside the walled garden from the road. It was guarded by three neat rows of trees and, of course, the wall from which it gained its name. Therefore, as gingerly as he was able, he climbed down from his curricle and made his way from the roadside, through the trees, and to the wall. Looking to his right and then his left, he sought the best approach.

Ah! There!

A few feet to his right was a section of the wall which was not so well-built as the rest and appeared to have foot and handholds in it. They would not afford him an easy ascent, but it was not as if he had to climb far to peek inside the garden. The wall which surrounded it was only an arm's length taller than he was, and he was not a short chap. Of course, he was not overly tall either, but he was not short.

"I am quite the right height, I would say," he muttered to himself as he placed his foot on a rock, testing its firmness before reaching upward with his hands. "Though, I will admit that being slightly taller would make for less climbing. Uh," he groaned as he pulled himself up with his sore arm. It was a particularly good thing that the wall was not taller. His bruised body was protesting even this short climb. Only one more step and pull were needed to crest the top of the wall. He placed his foot and grasped the edge of a stone above him. However, as he pressed up on his sore leg, his fingers lost their hold, sending him sliding down the rocky face of the wall.

"Can I not manage anything without injuring myself?" Crimson stained a torn stocking on his previously uninjured leg. He sat there on the ground, where he had come to rest with a great thud, looking up at the wall while tears spilled down his cheeks. Of all the stupid things, he was crying!

"Pull yourself together, man," he scolded. "It is just a scrape and a few more bruises." He tried to convince himself that that was all it was, but he knew it was more. It was pain to be sure, but it was also anger, the spinning in his head, and the aching of his heart. His life had always seemed a trifle charmed when he was younger and getting his way in all things, but now? Now, he knew the extent of that lie, and that mingled with his current frustrations and the necessary, though painful, trip he faced today were too much for him to keep contained. And so, the messy mix of emotions found their release in very ungentlemanly tears.

"Do you require assistance?"

Miles covered his face with his hands to hide the evidence of his unregulated emotions from whoever had approached. "No, I will be well in a moment."

"I doubt it," his would-be helper said, as he

grasped Miles under his arms to lift him from the ground.

"What? Wait just a moment!" Miles twisted away from the fellow as he brushed away his tears. However, both his ability to speak and move froze when he saw who it was.

"Mr. Chapman, I am not attempting to do you harm. In fact, I am trying to help you, even though you appear to be breaking into my garden."

"I... I..." Miles looked at the wall that was now behind him and then back at Mr. Wesley. What did one say to the father of the lady you loved but had abandoned when caught attempting to peek into his garden?

"You are not in Bath." Mr. Wesley handed him his handkerchief and shifted his eyes to the garden wall.

Miles was thankful for the attempt to salvage at least some of his dignity as he dried his face. "No, I am not, but I am on my way there."

"Climbing over my garden wall is not on any path to Bath." Mr. Wesley's lips twitched in amusement. "Now, if you can hobble on that bloody leg of yours, I suggest we walk to the road and then, get you to the house to see what can be done for you."

"But I must go to Bath," Miles protested.

"And leave a trail of blood? I think not."

"It is only a scrape." Surely, the bleeding would soon stop.

"You have several of those."

"I do."

"And I would like to know why."

And Miles would rather not explain them, which meant he needed to be on his way, for keeping his secret hidden when he felt as woozy and wobbly as he did would be nearly impossible.

"Are you just naturally clumsy?" Mr. Wesley asked.

"No, no, I am usually rather sure-footed."

"I suspected as much. Neither Charlotte nor Louisa have made mention of an inability to dance on your part. Now, before I help you into your carriage, you will promise me that you will return to the house with me." There was no amusement in Mr. Wesley's expression.

"Yes, sir, I will." How else was he supposed to reply to a demand from a gentleman whom he hoped to persuade to continue to consider him as a husband for his daughter?

"Good. You may climb into your curricle. I will stand here to make certain you do not topple out."

It was a good thing that Mr. Wesley was standing near because Miles did waver as he was ascending his vehicle. However, he did not fall and was soon seated with the ribbons grasped in his hand while Mr. Wesley assisted in turning the horse and carriage on the somewhat narrow road.

Turning down this lane to attempt a final glance at Charlotte had been a grave error, Miles thought as he followed Mr. Wesley to the driveway. And entering her house, as he was about to do, was most certainly not on his "things that will make leaving your heart behind to appease your father and keep the woman you love safe" list of things-to-do today.

However, by turning down this lane, injuring himself, and being discovered, entering the Wesleys' house had been added to his list since dashing off in his curricle to avoid entering the house seemed excessively silly and, more importantly, unlikely to work. Mr. Wesley had a horse with no carriage and could probably catch him. Besides all that, his body and head were hurting too much to be knocked around in riotous driving. Indeed, thanks to his sore body and head, he had never driven so slowly as he had today.

He shivered. The temperature seemed to be dipping despite the sun being bright.

"It is a rather cool day, is it not?" he asked as he sat in his carriage, attempting to delay the inevitable.

Mr. Wesley's head tipped. "Cool?"

Miles nodded and closed his eyes as the movement caused the spinning of his head to increase.

"We can discuss that when you are safely inside with a cup of tea to warm you."

"It is not cool?"

Mr. Wesley shook his head. "Not unless you have a fever."

Ah, yes, that did make sense. Why had he not thought of that? It was probably for the same reason he had thought trying to climb a stone wall when injured was a good idea. His brain was in a fog from a fever. He sighed and tossed his reins to a waiting groom before allowing Mr. Wesley to help him from his carriage. Travelling with a fever was definitely one of the least bright ideas he had ever had.

"I was surprised by the letter I received today," Mr. Wesley said as he entered the house.

Miles paused just outside the door. How had Mr. Wesley gotten that letter already? He had told Tom to keep it until he was an hour away from Oxford, which would have been just... He pulled out his watch.

"We were at the Levy's house. They are good friends of ours who live in town." Mr. Wesley stood in the entryway watching Miles. "My daughter wished for me to see you and assure her that you were not dying." His eyes roamed from Miles's head to his feet. "You seem somewhat alive to me." Mr. Wesley smirked and turned away to speak to his butler.

"We will have tea in my study, and a room for Mr. Chapman should be prepared. Also send a messenger to my study in fifteen minutes." He walked a few steps before stopping and turning back. "We will also require a cloth to tie up Mr. Chapman's leg and a bath to be drawn for him before he retires to bed."

"I cannot stay here," Miles said as he scurried behind Mr. Wesley.

"I will be the judge of that, and from the way your mind does not seem to be working so quickly as it has been wont to do in our other meetings, I have judged that you are not fit for travel. Your horse and carriage will be well-tended to until you are fit."

"But I cannot stay here."

Mr. Wesley smiled like a nursemaid placating a disgruntled child and waved Miles into the study ahead of him. "I am afraid you must."

Miles simply shook his head, which was still as bad an idea as it had been before. He held his head between his hands to stop the spinning he felt. It helped, but only marginally.

"Sit." Mr. Wesley commanded, and Miles obeyed. "You will stay, and you will be grateful that I am not disposed to seeing you pay for deserting my daughter."

Miles swallowed. "I was not deserting her."

"You have left school, which goes directly against one of the stipulations of our agreement for you to be allowed to present your offer." Mr. Wesley sat down behind his desk. "Explain."

The room felt excessively warm. Miles rubbed his hands on his breeches to dry them. "And if I do not?" he asked cautiously.

Mr. Wesley tipped his head and studied Miles. The clock ticked twenty-five times before he took an audible breath and spoke. "It is time to dismount the pig."

Miles's brow furrowed. What was the man talking about?

"Indeed, I think it is about time we had some ham for dinner and a rasher, or two, of bacon for breakfast. Your father has done enough."

He blinked. His father? Had Tom told Mr. Wesley about the current scheme which was afoot?

"Charlotte has reasoned out – based on the limited information in your letters," he placed two missives on his desk, "and what your friend refused to say – that your father has done something to precipitate this ruse of deserting my daughter." He sat back. "Tell me she is wrong."

It took only a moment for Miles to contemplate saying Charlotte was wrong. A good man did not prevaricate when it came to matters as important as questioning the quick wit of the lady he loved. "I cannot. However, I would also beg of you to just allow me to continue on my way and not explain the whole of the matter."

"Do you still wish to marry my daughter?"

That was not the reply he had expected. He eyed the man across from him warily. "Yes. With all that is within me I do, but not at the expense of her safety or that of my friend."

"I believe I have enough information about your character to allow you to present your offer and, if accepted, to set the date for whenever the two of you wish."

Miles closed his eyes and scrubbed his face. His fever must be worsening, for he had just imagined that Mr. Wesley had given him permission to marry Charlotte. Perhaps he should ask to see the apothecary.

"I had imagined you would look happier than you do to find out that I am no longer postponing my approval of your offer," Mr. Wesley said when Miles opened his eyes.

"You are accepting me? It is not just my fever making me delirious?" Delight began to bubble up within him.

Mr. Wesley chuckled. "I am accepting you on

one condition beyond my daughter's willingness to be your wife."

One condition? There was only one thing standing between him and his happy future? "Anything."

Mr. Wesley's smile turned somewhat sly. "You will explain, in detail, why you were appearing to desert both your education and my daughter. What has your father done?"

The reality of being Sir Allen's son came crashing down around Miles. He had forgotten for a moment about his father and the need to keep both Charlotte and Tom safe. "Anything but that." He rose on legs that felt as if they would crumble beneath him. He had to leave. "I cannot..." He shook his head as the finality of what he was doing clogged his throat, cutting off his words.

"Would you truly give Charlotte up so easily?"

"It is anything but easy," Miles protested. "My father is not a kind man, sir. I do not give up what I so desperately desire because it is easy." Did Mr. Wesley not understand that this trip to Bath was not one made for pleasure?

Their conversation paused as tea was brought in along with a cloth for Miles's leg, which had ceased bleeding some time ago, and a message was hastily written and sent out. Once the door closed behind Mr. Hillier, Mr. Wesley picked their discussion back up.

"How long will you allow your father to direct your life?"

"For as long as I must." It was not as if he wished to do as his father bid, but there was too much at stake not to.

"And how long is that? One year? Thirty? If your father has his way now, what is to prevent him from doing so again? Do you expect him to eventually relent from his position?"

Miles sank onto the chair from which he had risen. It was hopeless, was it not? He would never be free of his father, would he?

"Ask yourself this. What do you fear more: whatever you think your father might do or seeing Charlotte married to another?"

Mr. Wesley's pointed question found its mark, striking at not just the heart of the matter but piercing Miles's heart as well. "I do not care what my father might do to me. It is what he might do to Charlotte... and Tom."

"Tell me about it," Mr. Wesley pleaded. "Let me help you protect my daughter and your friend."

"It is my connection to you which poses the danger. That is why I must leave."

Mr. Wesley shook his head. "It is not the connection. It is the fact that you are not doing what he wishes. Do you think he will just allow you to take up your position with Mr. Norman without protest?"

That thought had truly never occurred to Miles.

"Stand your ground. Forge your own future. Be my son."

Miles looked at him in surprise. "Your son?"

"If Charlotte will have you, and I do think she will. I am not certain how you have swayed her opinion. However, since she is a lot like me, I will guess it is your stalwart character that will sacrifice for the welfare of a friend and your determination to do what you must to achieve what you wish, mixed with your tendency to be honest even when it shines a poor light on you." He shook his head. "I did not think you had such resolve in you. I had hoped you did, but I admit to being a trifle doubtful about my own instincts."

Mr. Wesley thought highly of him? Him? Miles

Chapman? The fellow who, until recently, had thought more about himself than anything else? "Are... are you certain? I have a whole cadre of faults. I am still in want of a goodly amount of improvement."

This was met with a chuckle. "Yes, I am certain. I could not ask for a better son than one who is willing to admit his deficits and seek improvement. Now, do we have an agreement? Will you stay here, tell me about what your father has done, and persuade my daughter to allow me to claim you as a son? I am not afraid of what your father might try. I am certain we can best him if we work together."

It was what he wanted more than anything, but... "I worry we cannot."

"That is understandable. Your father has been controlling and mean all your life. You cannot see this as I do. It just is not presently possible. Please, trust me. I am nothing like your father. I will never treat you meanly. Do we have an agreement?"

Miles looked at the ceiling and exhaled deeply. Those stupid tears were once again threatening, while hope mingled with fear and rose triumphant as he nodded his agreement.

# Chapter 12

He was handsome even when he was sleeping and had a scrape on one side of his face. But then, she had always found him handsome from the beginning. It had been his fine features that had first caught her eye, until his behaviour had put her off. That reprehensible, far-too-self-appreciating behaviour was no longer an issue, nor did she have those niggling, worrisome thoughts about how it was wrong to fall in love with a man purely because he was dashing. She was free to love him without reserve, for she had discovered he was more than a pretty face.

Charlotte kissed her fingers and touched Mr. Chapman's injured face gently.

His eyes opened a crack, and he smiled at her.

"Does it hurt terribly?" she whispered before placing the back of her hand against his forehead.

He was warm but not excessively so. His fever, which had been nearly gone yesterday morning when he had left Oxford, had come raging back by nightfall. It was good to see that it was not going to hang on stubbornly.

"No," he answered sleepily, allowing his eyes to fall shut.

"You do know that lying in your bed would be more restful, do you not?" She drew a stool close to the chair he sat in near the window in the sitting room that had always been hers and Louisa's and had only ever been for company when Mrs. Levy came to call.

"You could not sit by my bedside." His eyes remained closed. "And I am quite comfortable as I am."

He did look perfectly content, with his head resting against one wing of the chair's back and his legs propped up on a footstool. He wore only his shirt and breeches under his dressing gown, and his slippered feet stuck out from under the light blanket that was draped across him. If Charlotte were being honest with herself, then she had to admit that she was happy to be able to sit next to him.

"Do you need anything?" she asked.

"Just you." He held his hand out in her direction, and when she took it, he sighed.

Father had told her about the discussion he had had with Mr. Chapman yesterday. Therefore, she did not even feel a twinge of guilt for being improper and holding his hand. After all, they were nearly betrothed. She had only to wait until he was well enough to make his offer. How strange it was that, in so short a time, the thought of marrying him no longer caused her a drop of confusion but instead stirred excitement within her.

He opened his eyes. "Were you in the garden today?"

"I was. It is a bright and warm day. However, the breeze is strong, so doing much more than walking or sitting is difficult. The pages of a book would not lie still, and an easel would have wobbled. Indeed, keeping my bonnet in place while walking was a challenge."

"I wanted to take a walk with you in the garden, but your father would not allow it."

"He is excessively wise. You are not well enough for a walk in the garden. Maybe in a day or two."

He chuckled. "That is exactly what your father said. He told me you and he are a lot alike."

"We are." Her mother had always called them her two peas in a pod. It was lovely to be likened to her father, for he was a wonderful man. However, it also meant that he often knew what she was thinking nearly before she had thought it herself. It both kept her out of trouble and from fun when she was a child.

Mr. Chapman's expression grew serious. "He is an exceptionally good man. You have been blessed to have him as your father. I hope I can be as good as he." He squeezed her hand. "You deserve so much better than me."

"Do not say so," she scolded. "I know what you did for me at *The Drunken Boar*. My father told me." Even thinking about the incident made her cheeks warm. She had been thoroughly horrified and mortified to hear the details.

"Any gentleman would do the same for the lady he loved."

"But it was not any gentleman. It was you. And it was not just some lady. It was me."

"I would do far more for you."

"I know." And she did know that now. "My

opinion of you has changed quite a bit recently." Her heart thumped at the admission. "But, then, I also understand more about why you were as you were. Not that I approve of how you were."

"Neither do I. Now that I can see myself for the arrogant idiot I was, I disapprove of me most vigorously. I will not be so again." His eyes closed again, and he stifled a yawn.

"You should sleep."

His hand tightened on hers when she tried to withdraw it.

"Do not leave me. I want to talk to you. We still know so little about one another – although I shall probably always feel that way until I know everything there is to know about you." His smile was as sweet as his words.

Charlotte was not given to fits of swooning at romantic words or actions, and yet, it took some effort to not sigh as Louisa would. Instead, she said the sensible thing. "You are tired. That can wait."

"I do not want to wait." He blew out a breath and opened his eyes again. "I fear my father will find a way to take you from me."

"I do not understand him," she admitted. "I have tried, but I cannot. It is not natural how he treats you or your family." Every time she had contemplated Sir Allen, her heart had broken a little bit more for the son he was currently casting aside like some unwanted piece of china. And just like a china bowl, the gentleman holding her hand bore cracks and chips from being treated roughly. Thankfully, he did not seem to be shattered.

"I do not understand it either, nor do I feel equal to attempting such a feat. I wish I could forget him."

"But you cannot."

He shook his head. "No, I cannot. I fear he will always be a part of me – of us?" His eyes when he looked at her held as much uncertainty as his voice.

"Of us?" she repeated, her heart picking up its pace. "Do explain." Was he planning to propose?

"Has your father told you that he gave me permission to ask you to marry me?"

She nodded. He was. He was not going to wait until he was well before offering for her.

"Will you? I promise to work every day to be worthy of you. I love you so dearly."

He had said that before, all that time ago in Bath when she was staying with her grandparents. However, she had not believed him at that time. She had thought him merely infatuated, but she did not question him any longer. It was true that they still had much to learn about each other, but she knew enough to know that his words were true and echoed her own feelings for him. He was not just a handsome face that made her heart flutter. Once his admiration of himself had been stripped away, what remained was a gentleman of promising character who was passionate about his friends and his interests.

She drew a breath and willed herself to hold his gaze. "I love you," she whispered. She had only ever made that confession aloud to her darkened bedroom before. She had admitted to caring for him very much to all her family and even Mrs. Levy and Mr. Green, but she had never said she loved him to anyone until now. She had been saving that word just for him.

"You love me?" His smile was brilliant.

She nodded. "I most certainly do. Therefore, it would be excessively silly for me not to marry you, and I am a mostly sensible lady."

"If you are agreeing to marry me, I might have to question your sensibleness, but I will refrain from doing so until we are husband and wife. I would not wish to do anything to make you change your mind."

Charlotte laughed. "You may question, but you will find you are wrong."

"Will I, indeed?"

She leaned forward and lifted his hand to her lips to kiss it. "Do you remember the assembly at Bath where you found me, and I nearly fainted away at the surprise?"

"I do."

"Well, before I nearly fainted, I was talking to Mr. Norman while I was attempting to avoid being seen by you, and I admitted to him that I was afraid that I loved a popinjay – which is something a sensible lady does not do. And do you know what he said?"

"I am sure I could not even hazard a guess."

"He told me that the only remedy was to attempt to find someone to take your place in my admiration. If I could do that, then I was right, but if I could not, then I had to admit that even a sensible person can be wrong."

"Have you tried to replace me?" he asked in surprise.

"No. Not even once. I could think of no one else,

and when I received your letter yesterday, I knew, beyond a shadow of a doubt, that I wanted no one but you. So, you see, Mr. Chapman, I was wrong, and when a sensible lady is wrong, she seeks to make things right. Therefore, both my being wrong and my willingness to accept your offer prove that I am, in fact, a sensible lady who loves a wonderful gentleman who is as handsome as any popinjay could ever hope to be, but who is also so much more."

His brow was creased with confusion. "I am not certain I followed all your reasoning, but I will allow it to be true anyway."

"You need rest." His eyelids appeared heavy.

"I would like to kiss you, but it must wait until I am well."

Charlotte's cheeks grew rosy, and she looked down at their joined hands. "The more you rest, the faster you will be well."

"Do you mean –"

"Do not ask me what I mean. It is unsettlingly enough that I should say what I said."

He chuckled. "Very well, my proper love. I will not ask you if you meant you wished for me to kiss you."

The door to the sitting room opened, and Charlotte turned to see who had entered.

"Is this not a cozy scene?" her father teased.

"They have been all that is proper," Charlotte's maid, who was sitting in the corner working on some stitching and playing chaperone, inserted.

"I would expect nothing less."

"She has accepted me," Mr. Chapman said brightly.

"That is wonderful news. Much better than the news in this letter." He brought the chair which stood next to the writing desk over to where they were and sat down. "Mr. Eyers was not bluffing. I am guessing that it was the redirection of your things to my home rather than to Bath which forced his hand as we expected might happen. The magistrate was informed this morning of a theft of an expensive bottle of wine and some monies. Both you and Mr. Green were named in the accusation."

Charlotte's throat seemed to climb into her throat. Accused of theft? That was no trifling matter.

"But we took nothing," Mr. Chapman cried. "In fact, we were not even in Mr. Eyers' room."

"I know, and I am on my way to town to see that all is set to right. I will begin with Mr. Eyers, but if he will not listen to me and rescind his accusation, then I will be forced to plead your case with the magistrate."

"Will that be enough? What will become of Mr. Green?" Charlotte asked. "Does Louisa know?"

"No, but I will tell both she and your mother before I leave. I am hopeful that a few conversations and a bit of money can clear this up. Mr. Chapman's father might not approve of my connections, but I can assure you my ties include some powerful people. One of them is the magistrate. He is the fellow who dared me to sing in the quadrangle. It is also he who wrote to me about the accusations. I think our chances are good. I would not have you worry too much, but you needed to be aware of the situation." He stood. "May I share your good news with your mother and sister before I leave? It would give them something happy to think about rather than fretting too much over this situation."

"Of course, you may."

He kissed the top of Charlotte's head and shook Mr. Chapman's uninjured hand. "I would suggest," he said before leaving, "that you choose a date that is close. I think the sooner the matter is irreversibly settled, the better. Sir Allen cannot prevent what has already happened."

# Chapter 13

For two days, the Wesley home waited to hear what had transpired in Oxford. Some of that time was spent pleasantly employed in discussing wedding breakfast details, while other periods were spent in quiet and anxious anticipation. Wedding plans could only truly move forward if the groom was not going to find himself in jail, transported, or worse.

"I see no mention of anything regarding you in the paper," Mrs. Wesley said to Miles when he entered the breakfast room on Monday morning, the day when they expected Mr. Wesley to return. "You look well."

"Aside from the bruises and scrapes?" Miles asked. He liked Mrs. Wesley nearly as much as he liked her husband. She was practical but not without a tendency to get carried off by fits of fancy with her youngest daughter now and again.

"Yes, well, besides that," she replied. "You seem to have the appropriate amount of colour in your cheeks. Do you feel well?

"I do."

After settling into his place beside her at the breakfast table, he placed his hand on Charlotte's left forearm and getting her attention, smiled his greeting. Seeing her each morning and as often as he wished during the day was wonderful.

"Does the pain linger still?" Mrs. Wesley asked.

"My shoulder is still somewhat limited in motion, but my legs are much improved." Being still for several days would do that for sore legs. "Not that I will be climbing any steep hills –"

"Or garden walls," Louisa inserted with a laugh.

"No. I will not be climbing any walls at all for some time."

"Do you plan to climb walls in the future?"

It was entertaining to startle Louisa and cause her to ask such questions. "I have no plans to climb any walls ever. However, one never knows when it might become necessary."

Louisa opened her mouth as if to protest, but

then she closed it again as her eyebrows raised and she nodded. "That does make sense."

"Oh!" Mrs. Wesley gasped. "I spoke too soon."

"About what, Mother?" Charlotte asked.

"There is a bit in the paper about Miles."

Though the thought of being mentioned in the paper made his heart beat uncomfortably, Miles could not help smiling at Mrs. Wesley's use of his name. She had insisted that, if he was going to be her son, she was going to call him by his Christian name, and he had willingly acquiesced. He was delighted beyond any description to be considered part of the Wesley family.

"Well, not precisely about Miles," she added.

His heartbeat slowed a pace, but only just.

"However," she continued, "it does concern him indirectly."

"How so?" Miles asked. "Though I quake to know."

"No one will be putting you in the stocks, but your father will be less than pleased." Her eyes sparkled with amusement. She had been quite vocal about what she thought should happen to Sir Allen when she had arrived home and found his son sick with a fever and then discovered the cause of his injuries. Her opinion of Sir Allen had only sunk further when she heard about the charges being laid against Tom and Miles. Therefore, whatever was in the paper must be something that would make his father furious since it seemed to please Mrs. Wesley so much.

Miles pushed his plate away. His appetite had fled because spending a day in the stocks with rotten food being hurled at him would not be less pleasant than dealing with his irate father.

She covered her lips and attempted to conceal a laugh as she silently read what was written in the paper.

"Mother, how can you laugh about such a thing as news that will make Miles's father angry?" Charlotte chided.

"Oh, Sir Allen is going to be more than angry. He will be beside himself." This time a giggle did escape her as she handed the paper to Charlotte. "I would read it aloud, dear, but I fear I will not be able to do so and keep my composure. I do apologize for my mirth, Miles."

Charlotte lifted the paper and began reading the portion of the paper to which her mother had directed her.

*Interesting things are afoot for a particular baronet who has been known to frequent our town to visit his son, who was, until recently, a student at one of our numerous colleges. Many of us know this baronet as a goodly sort of fellow who appears to be well-established in society and of the highest and best pedigree. But it is not so. His true heritage has been lying hidden, cleverly tucked away, until it was recently revealed to me through an anonymous source, who knows the baronet well and whose tales cannot be questioned because of the tightness of the connection. It seems that while Sir A has been adamantly opposing a match between his son and a lady with ties to trade in her family history, I have proof in my possession of the lineage of Sir A, which traverses, not just through trade, but through the oldest and most shadowy of trades, plied in secret by ladies of ill repute. Yes, readers, I am saying that Sir A's grandmother was first his grandfather's mistress before he made an honest woman of her shortly before his child was born. It seems that Sir A, for all his gallantry, fares no better, and likely far worse, than a young woman whose long-ago relations sold respectable goods.*

"Oh, my!" Louisa cried.

"Oh, my, indeed." Charlotte looked from the paper to Miles.

"My great-grandmother was a prostitute?" That was a surprising secret, to say it gently.

"That is what this says," Charlotte answered.

Miles sank back in his chair. His father would be livid when he heard about this bit of tattle in the paper. Hopefully, he would not think that Miles was the source of the information. He rubbed his chin. Who would know such secrets? Unless... His head tipped. "Do you suppose it is a fabrication?"

Charlotte's shoulders lifted and lowered in a shrug.

"Whether it is true or not, it will rile your father. His pristine image has been thoroughly marred." Mrs. Wesley took up her teacup. "I know it is not right to think so, so do not scold me, Charlotte, but it is no more than he deserves for spreading rumours about you and Miles."

"One reaps what he sows," Louisa said. "That is what the parson says."

"That is true," Mrs. Wesley agreed. "In light of that, I shall refuse to feel bad for not pitying the man." She looked at Miles. "I do feel the weight of it on your account."

"I am only disturbed by it because I fear my father will think I am the unnamed source."

Charlotte sucked in a quick breath.

Mrs. Wesley's cup returned to the table quickly. "That is a very troubling thought, indeed!" She rose from her place at the table and went to the window to look out towards the stables. "I do wish Mr. Wesley was here."

"As do I!" Louisa cried.

Apparently, now was one of the times when two of the Wesley ladies were going to fly into the rafters if allowed. Miles cast about in his mind for something he could say to put them at ease, but to be honest, his mind was just as troubled as theirs.

"I do not care if your father thinks it is you," Charlotte said with a meaningful look, that he likely should understand but did not.

"Not care!" her mother cried.

Charlotte's lips twitched.

Ah! She was directing her mother and sister. Relief washed over him. He could focus on simply containing his own anxieties and not worry about those of his soon-to-be relations.

"I shudder to think what he will do that he has not already done," Mrs. Wesley added.

"Oh, it is a most dreadful prospect, Lottie. I do

not see how you cannot care about that!" Louisa agreed.

"No, it is not a completely horrid prospect." Charlotte turned to Miles and took hold of his right hand. "Do you not remember how you said your father was cowed into proper behaviour at your sister's wedding breakfast?"

"I do, but those were only threats of damage to his reputation. This is a step further."

"Perhaps this will teach him that the threats were not empty."

He shook his head. Perhaps if his father were a quicker study, but Miles knew that his father was excessively stubborn. He doubted that Sir Allen would learn anything from this.

"Must we always live in fear of him, then?"

Charlotte's whispered words struck Miles with a force greater than he imagined Haworth's fist would impart.

"I do not wish to," he admitted. "But what can I do? I do not care about myself so much as I do you."

"Would you take back the punch you landed on Mr. Haworth?"

His brow furrowed. "No, but I do not see how that applies."

"This article is a blow." She said no more. Her expectant look was very similar to the one her father used.

"But it is not one which I landed."

She pressed her lips together and continued to look at him silently, though he was certain it was taking some effort for her to do so. His lips curved upward as understanding began to dawn on him. If he would not regret hitting Haworth then...

"However," he continued, "if it were of my doing, I would not regret it."

Her smile was the best reward he had ever received for answering a question – even if that question had not actually been asked.

He looked at Mrs. Wesley and Louisa. "Charlotte is correct. I do not care if my father thinks it was me who gave that information to the paper. He should be knocked about for his behaviour."

He pulled his plate back towards himself. His appetite had returned.

"I only wish I had known that family secret," Miles continued, "so that I could have shared it long ago when he first began the rumours that put Charlotte's reputation in jeopardy."

Charlotte squeezed his hand and then placed a

kiss on his cheek. It was something she had done several times over the past few days. His hand had also received a few kisses. And she always blushed very prettily after being so forward – just like she was doing now. Unfortunately, his lips had yet to be blessed with one of her kisses. Soon. He was well enough now.

He pulled his eyes away from her. "Please, do not let my moment of worry interrupt our breakfast," he said as he skewered a piece of ham and chuckled at the appropriateness of that item of food for this morning's events. The pig was no longer able to be ridden. This challenge would be met head-on. "I wonder if this means my father will pay us a call?"

"He might," Mr. Wesley stood at the door to the breakfast room.

"Father!" Louisa cried. "We were just wishing you were here."

Mr. Wesley crossed the room and kissed his wife before taking his place at the table.

"Was your trip a success?" Mrs. Wesley asked. "Or are we spiriting our daughter and son away to the continent or some other far-flung destination?"

He chuckled. "Have we set a date for the wedding?"

"How can we, when we do not know what will become of Miles?" his wife asked.

"You may select whichever date you would like," he replied as his cup was being filled with coffee by a footman. "It seems the charges were a misunderstanding." His left eyebrow cocked. "Mr. Eyers consulted with his informant and discovered his information was faulty." Again, the man chuckled. "He did so because he decided that he wished to keep his position. However," he looked at Miles, "he will not be your tutor for your final term."

"His final term?" Charlotte asked before Miles's mind could formulate and utter the same words. "He left school."

"Many fellows do between terms. He is just tardy in returning because of an illness and possible marriage, or so all the appropriate people have been told." He settled back in his chair with his cup of coffee and a smile upon his face. "As I said, my connections are far better than Sir Allen might think possible."

"How did you do all this?" Mrs. Wesley asked.

Mr. Wesley took a sip of his coffee before

answering. "A little cash as a reward for compliance, and then, a mention of the possible termination of Mr. Eyers' position. It was a magic combination. I have never seen a fellow so willing to retract his accusations." He sipped his coffee again. "It was enough to make me question the man's credentials, but Mr. Green assures me that Mr. Eyers has never withheld any information in an attempt to do Miles harm."

Miles blinked. He had never considered that his tutor would attempt to sabotage his education.

"Miles will not be the only one with a new tutor. Mr. Green – Tom – will also be under the tutelage of another since his father was in agreement with me about ending all association with Mr. Eyers. Mr. Green – Tom's father – arrived yesterday."

Tom's father was in town? Poor Tom. Miles could only imagine the reprimanding Tom had received for having insisted on remaining Miles's friend contrary to his father's advice.

"I have invited both he and his son to dine with us tomorrow."

Miles swallowed.

"I assure you," Mr. Wesley continued, "that the elder Mr. Green is not furious any longer. In fact, he is desirous that I extend his thanks to you for your willingness to give up your schooling for his son's protection."

"You told him about that?"

Mr. Wesley nodded. "I told him everything you have been through recently and how much I approved of you."

"You did?"

"I did. He was quite impressed." Mr. Wesley smirked. "It seemed to me, when he first arrived, that his opinion of you was rather poor. Therefore, I thought it best to share all I knew."

"Thank you," Miles said. "For all of it – seeing to the charges and my schooling and convincing Tom's father that I am not a poor choice as a friend." Had anyone ever seen to his care in such a fashion?

Mr. Wesley returned his cup to the table and leaned forward with his gaze intently focused on Miles. "This is what a father should do for his child. It is his duty in life to see to the welfare of his wife and family, ensuring that they are safe and well-provided-for, even if it comes at great expense and effort. And, in my opinion, the best fathers lead by example."

Miles understood the admonition. "It is how I plan to be."

"I thought as much," Mr. Wesley said with a smile as he returned to his cup of coffee. "Now, I heard something about Charlotte being correct – which does not surprise me – but I am curious as to what family secret Miles wishes he had shared with the paper."

"Have you not read the paper today?" Mrs. Wesley asked in surprise.

"I was in a rush to get home to you, and reading on horseback is not so easy as it is in a carriage."

Louisa reached across the table and snatched the paper from Charlotte. "You must read it," she said to her father. "Sir Allen's grandmother was a..." she lowered her voice, "a lady of the night. It is right here." She pointed to the article her father needed to read, which he did rather quickly.

"Well," he said with a sigh once he had finished, "when you couple this with the letter that I had Mr. Eyers write to Sir Allen, informing him that he would no longer be a tutor to Mr. Chapman and that Miles was, in fact, returning to school, I believe we should prepare for a visit. How quickly can we arrange a wedding breakfast?"

"No," Miles said quickly before anyone else could answer. He was not going to run from his father. "I think it would be best if we married after my term is complete."

"But your father..." Charlotte said.

"Will likely be here before we can sort out the dishes to be served." He looked at the startled faces of his new family. "Believe me when I say I would rather marry tomorrow than wait. However, Charlotte was correct. I will not alter my plans to avoid him and his scheming, and to be honest, I fear I would not be able to focus on my studies if I had a wife." His ears burned at the admission. "Delaying our wedding will also give me time to gather information from Mr. Norman about my finances and what housing can be found for Charlotte and me." He had meant his promise to Mr. Wesley that he would be the sort of husband and father who put the welfare of his family before his own desires. He turned back to Charlotte. "What do you say?"

Thankfully, she smiled, easing his fears that his determination to be what he should be would make her unhappy.

"I say, Mr. Chapman, that it sounds like an excessively sensible plan. I will marry you whenever you deem best — tomorrow or at the end of your term or even at the end of the year my father had required at first."

"I am not that sensible," Miles inserted, causing both Mr. and Mrs. Wesley to chuckle.

"The point is, I will marry you, and I will stand by your side now as I will then," Charlotte concluded.

It really was too bad they were in the breakfast room with the full family in attendance because Miles was well enough to kiss Charlotte, and such a reply seemed to demand such a response. However, they were not alone, and so Miles satisfied himself with kissing her fingers.

"The weather is perfect this morning. In fact, it is an ideal day for a stroll in the garden, Charlotte," Mr. Wesley said. "Miles seems to be finished eating and looking well. I think he would benefit from a walk in the sunshine." He winked at Miles. "I would not be surprised if there are a few new buds or flowers to discover."

"Oh! I will join you," Louisa cried.

"No, you will not," her mother answered.

"Why?" Louisa was a quick one to pout.

"Charlotte and Miles need no chaperone. They

are betrothed after all." She cast a sly look in Miles's direction. "Do not tell me you have already forgotten that Mr. Green and his father are coming to dinner tomorrow. You do wish to help me plan that, do you not?"

Louisa gasped. "I had forgotten!"

"It is a good thing one of us remembered," Mrs. Wesley said while looking at Miles and tipping her head toward the door.

He was not going to wait for any further instructions. As Louisa began listing the items she thought they should have for dinner, Miles rose, offered his hand to Charlotte, and escorted her from the room. Then, just as soon as the door to the breakfast room closed behind him, he pulled Charlotte into his embrace and, finally, kissed her.

# Chapter 14

Charlotte sat in her favourite place to sit in the morning – on the small wall that surrounded the fountain in the walled garden. She lifted her face to the sunshine and drew in a deep breath. It was such a peaceful morning. All seemed right in her world. There were clouds hanging around the edges, but at this moment, they were far enough away that she could do no more than give them a cursory thought. She took one more deep, refreshing breath of the spring air before turning her attention to the note which was tucked inside her book.

"Have you not yet finished the Dashwoods' story?" her father teased as he approached.

It had been in this very spot where not many days ago, she had confessed to rereading Miles's first letter to her father. That letter was still tucked between the pages of this favoured book, but it was not that letter which she was reading.

She lifted the missive that lay on top of the page, to which her book was open, and held it so her father could see that she was reading a letter but not so he could read the words contained within it. "I find that one gains a deeper understanding and appreciation for a particular piece of writing when one reads it more than once."

Her father chuckled as he took a place next to her. "Is it not silly to reread a letter?"

That is how she had felt the last time she had been found rereading Mr. Chapman's letter. "A wise man, whom I love dearly, once told me it was not, and I choose to believe him."

Her father sighed. "What will I do without you around here?"

"I am not leaving until June."

"Six weeks is not an exceedingly long time, but this is how it is supposed to be. A parent does his job until his job is complete."

"Your duty as my father will never be complete." She rested her head on his shoulder.

"My duty is changing significantly. I am no longer the one to whom you are to turn with your problems, and I will not be the one to enjoy an early morning conversation with you. Those things and so many more will soon be the responsibility and pleasure of your husband."

Charlotte could not deny that things in her life were shifting. "But it is not all sorrow, is it?" She would hate to think that, by finding her own happiness, she was causing sadness for her father.

"No, not at all. It is an odd mix of satisfaction and melancholy. One must focus on the satisfaction. You are marrying well. A few weeks ago, when we met like this after your return from Bath, I would not have said so with so much confidence as I now have. Miles struck me as a young man with great potential, but I questioned his determination."

"So did I."

"Did you?"

"I did. I thought his affection for me might be fleeting. I never imagined that he truly loved me or that his feelings ran so deep that he would give up everything, including me, to see that I was safe."

"That was surprising," her father admitted, "but pleasantly so. The other thing which has been delightfully unexpected is how quickly you shifted from running from him to wishing to never be parted from him."

It had been a rapid change in her thinking, which must have looked even hastier to those who were not privy to her inner contemplations. "I never disliked him completely."

"Did you not? I had thought that you nearly despised him. That is why I was so willing to let you go to visit your grandparents."

"I found him handsome, attractive even, but he was so arrogant and thought only of himself – or so I thought. It seemed foolish to even entertain the notion of liking him. Sensible young ladies do not wish for silly beaus."

"But?" her father prompted when she paused to think about how she had been in such a hurry to be away from Miles and the confusing things he had made her feel.

"But, Miles is not silly. Not at his heart. He was misguided, I will grant that, and he was indeed too full of his own importance. However, that was not all he was, and I shall always be grateful to a pig for showing me that. For, a gentleman who thinks only of himself and naught else, one who is rotten through and through, does not protect a friend by making a fool of himself."

"And now that you know that, your heart and your head can agree." It was not asked as a question but stated as a logical and completely understood conclusion. This was just another way that she and her father were alike. Their methods of reasoning often took the same path.

"Yes, both my head and my heart love him."

Her father sighed again. "That is my reward for seeing to my duty as your father. You are not just marrying well, you are also happy."

"Very."

"I will not keep you from your letter. My coffee awaits me." He stood. "Is this the same letter that you were reading the last time we discussed Miles here?"

She shook her head. "I found this one in my room this morning. It had been slipped under my door sometime while I was sleeping."

"Then, you are not rereading?"

She smiled sheepishly. "I read it twice while dressing."

Her father chuckled. "I hope you enjoy it as much this time as you did on each of the previous perusals." And then, he left her by herself to reread Miles's words of endearment.

How could one not enjoy being called the delight of my heart or hearing her kiss referred to as *a precious treasure that soothes my soul and binds me to you like bands of the strongest iron?* He really could write poetry. That was still something that startled her. There were depths to him which had not yet been plumbed. She doubted he was even aware of some of those depths, and it was going to be her joy to discover them with him.

Upon hearing footsteps, she looked up from her fourth reading of his letter to find Miles approaching. He was only limping the tiniest amount.

"Good morning, my love," he called.

"Good morning." She closed her book and rose from her place.

"You may continue reading," he offered. "I would be content to sit and watch you or listen to you read aloud." He offered her his arm, and she took it.

"I was not reading my book, and I would like to walk with you."

"I am happy to hear that last bit, but why were you not reading your book? Is it dull? There have been many which I have been required to read that could put anyone to sleep. I do not know how such dreadful bits of boredom have become revered as texts that everyone must read to be thought well-educated."

She laughed lightly at his way of describing the books he did not enjoy. "This book is not dreadful in any fashion. It is actually quite delightful."

"Indeed?" his tone was suffused with interest. "Then you shall have to tell me about it, but not until after you have satisfied my curiosity about why you were not reading such a delightful book."

"I found it paled in comparison to a letter that I found lying just inside my bedroom door this morning."

"How intriguing!" he cried. "Do tell me all about it."

This was the charming liveliness that she had watched at several soirees and which had been missing from him for the past while – since his arrival in Bath, to be exact. She had missed it. That fact no longer made her question her sense. It confirmed to her that she loved every bit of the gentleman on whose arm she walked.

"I do believe it was written by a poet, for it was very charmingly done."

"A poet, you say?"

"Mmm-hmm."

"Would I know him?"

"Intimately."

"And he is sending you letters in the night?"

"So it would seem."

"Shall I tell him to cease? I could call him out if need be."

Charlotte chuckled. "No, I never wish for him to cease telling me of his love for me."

They had reached the arbour at the end of the walled garden, just before the wall redirected whoever was on this path to turn onto another.

"And why would that be?"

He had pulled her into his embrace just as he had yesterday when they had left the breakfast room. She was certain she would never grow tired of being held as he held her now.

"Because, being a sensible sort of lady, I like to be reminded of the truth of a matter."

He shook his head. "You are no flirt, Miss Wesley."

It was true. Flirting was something Louisa did.

It was not something Charlotte had ever wished to do – until now. "Then, Mr. Chapman, you shall have to teach me."

"That was much better, and it would be my pleasure, so long as you promise to never flirt with anyone but me."

"I cannot think of another person in all the world with whom I would even dare to think about flirting." She lifted onto her toes and placed a kiss on his lips. "I love you."

"How did I get to be so fortunate as to be loved by a lady like you?" He kissed her in return.

"You rode a pig to save your friend from embarrassment."

"That is why you love me?"

Charlotte shook her head. "That is when I stopped trying to not fall in love with you. I saw your heart in that story, and it spoke of the good man who lay hidden behind a popinjay's façade. Kiss me."

"Gladly."

Once again, he lowered his lips to hers as he had done more than once yesterday, and just like the first time he had kissed her in the hallway, her heart and body thrilled at the touch. Her arms held him closely, and she was once again amazed at how utterly proper it felt to be kissing him.

"You make me wonder what I was thinking to put our marriage off until June," he said when he finally broke their kiss.

"You were proving yourself as a gentleman worthy of a wife."

"I really was not looking for a sensible answer," he grumbled.

"Then, what were you hoping for?"

"I do not know. Perhaps that you would try to convince me to marry you sooner." He kissed her lightly again. "Doing what is sensible and right is not always easy."

"No, it is not." She could feel her cheeks warming. "Truth be told, at first, I was a trifle disappointed you wished to wait, but then, your explanation..." She sighed. "It made me feel... proud of you." She smoothed his hair over his ear with her right hand. "Proud to be the one you chose. I am content to wait." She smiled at him. "But not without a kiss now and again."

Thankfully, he obliged her with one more kiss before releasing her and suggesting they needed to return to the house. Arm in arm, they took a lazy stroll around the garden while Charlotte indulged in sharing Marianne and Elinor's story with him.

"I like the colonel," he said when she had completed her tale, "and that Edward fellow. However, the brother and his wife..." He shook his head. "It is very like life, is it not? There are those who behave nobly and those who are disgraceful."

"It is very like life."

"I have not decided how to proceed with my father," he said as they approached the fountain. "I spent a good amount of time lying in my bed and staring at the ceiling last night while trying to determine what I should do. Part of me feels as if I should make the first move rather than just waiting for him to strike, and part of me feels as if I should just wait to see what he does." He glanced at her. "I feel foolish asking for your guidance, but your father suggested I should."

"Did you talk to him about this?"

"I did. Before I came out to the garden. But he would not give me an answer other than to return to him if you and I could not devise a plan together."

"Why do you feel foolish asking for my advice?"

That thought made her bristle a bit, but she was not one to react without some thought.

His shoulders lifted and lowered in a shrug. "Should I not know the answer on my own? Am I not supposed to know how to steer a family? Is this just another area where I fall short because my father never taught me to be anything but a gentleman who looks good and does his bidding?"

Ah! It was not that he did not wish for her counsel. It was that he did not wish to appear lacking.

"I think your thoughts about waiting to see what he does is best. Return to school. Study and do well. And then, marry me and take up your profession. Live your life as you wish, and deal with anything he might do as it arises. Do not give him precedence. Is there a better way to deal a blow to a man, such as your father, than to go about life as if he does not matter?"

They walked on a pace in silence. From the way Miles's brow was furrowed, she guessed he was thinking about what she had said. Eventually, she was proven correct.

"I had not considered the fact that doing nothing more than what I planned to do was a significant blow. I thought that it might be seen as cowering or avoiding the problem of my father. However, to answer your question, I cannot think of anything that would irritate him more."

"Then, we are agreed? We will do nothing more than we are currently doing?"

His smile was answer enough, but she waited until he had assured her that they were agreed before she spoke further.

"Thank you for asking my opinion. I am happy to help you with all that I can."

"You do not care that I did not know the answer on my own?"

She shook her head. "Not at all."

He expelled a great breath. "That is excellent news." He followed her into the house.

"Is it settled?" Mr. Wesley asked when the two of them entered the breakfast room.

"Is what settled?" the ever-curious Louisa asked.

"A matter that is of no importance to you," her father replied, causing her to scowl.

"It is settled," Miles answered as he settled into his chair.

"I am happy to hear it," Mr. Wesley said.

"I dislike secrets," Louisa muttered.

"Drink your tea, dear." Mrs. Wesley gave her

youngest daughter a pointed look that Charlotte knew meant to keep quiet. Thankfully, Louisa obeyed without protest.

Mr. Wesley winked at his wife, she smiled in return, and breakfast proceeded without incident until Mr. Hillier entered.

"I do apologize for interrupting your breakfast, but there are relations of Mr. Chapman here, demanding to see him without delay."

"At this hour?" Mrs. Wesley asked in surprise.

"Yes, madame."

"Is it my father?" Miles asked.

"Yes, sir. Your father and your brother."

Charlotte saw Miles's shoulders lift as he drew a breath, and she took his hand, causing him to smile at her.

"I have not finished my breakfast. Is there a room where they can wait?" He looked to Mr. Wesley for direction.

"The blue drawing room should do."

"You may offer them tea," Mrs. Wesley added.

"Very good. I will see to it."

"Throw them from the house if they give you any trouble, Hillier," Mr. Wesley added. "They can wait on the drive if they prefer." He nodded to the footmen near the sideboard to follow the butler from the room.

"Well done," Charlotte whispered.

"Thank you."

He was standing his ground, but to Charlotte, he appeared to be excessively uneasy.

"Would you care for a second cup of tea and perhaps another plate of food?" Mrs. Wesley asked with a smile.

"No, I believe finishing what I have will be struggle enough," Miles admitted.

"There is no need to hurry." Her left eyebrow arched wickedly, and her lips pursed as if holding back her mirth. "No need at all."

Once again, Charlotte squeezed Miles's hand. "She is right."

"She often is," Mr. Wesley inserted. "See to him when you are ready and not a minute sooner."

Ten minutes passed with extraordinarily little conversation. Then, even though, he had not finished all that was on his plate, Miles stood.

"I believe I shall see to the issue and have it done with now," he said.

Charlotte stood up next to him.

"It might be best if I go alone."

"I meant it when I said I will stand with you. Please?"

"He will be unpleasant."

"I know."

"I do not want you to be hurt by his actions or his words."

"I know."

Mr. Wesley stood. "I will join the two of you because I am Charlotte's father."

"Are you both certain?" Miles asked.

"Yes," father and daughter said in unison.

And so, Charlotte took Miles's arm and, with her heart beating fast and loud, left the breakfast room to confront whatever lay before them in the drawing room.

# Chapter 15

Miles paused outside the drawing room door to attempt one last time to settle his nerves before facing his father. He had not seen the man since Belle's wedding, and that encounter had been an ugly one. However, most of his father's displeasure had been focused on Belle and Mr. Norman then. Today, he, alone, would be the one to bear the full force of his father's wrath.

"It is about time," Miles's father said when Miles entered the room. "I was beginning to wonder if the servants around here knew how to perform their duties." His lips curled in distaste as he flicked his gaze to Charlotte and her father. "I do not need to speak to anyone else."

"That is inconsequential." Miles attempted to sound confident, though he was feeling anything but. "This is Mr. Wesley's home and Charlotte will be my wife. It is best if they hear all you have to say. It will save me the trouble of relating it all to them later." He turned from his father. "Mr. Wesley, Charlotte, this is my father, Sir Allen Chapman, and my brother, Mr. Sidney Chapman."

Miles turned his attention back to his father and brother. "With what may I be of service?"

"Are you not going to introduce these people to me?" Sir Allen said with no little amount of indignation.

"No," Miles replied as he took a seat and everyone else followed. "I am certain you can figure out who each is." And he was not about to give his father an opportunity to be any ruder than he was already being.

Sir Allen huffed. "You were raised to be more proper than this." His eyes moved to Charlotte. "It is the influence of the company you keep."

"I am certain you are correct, Father," Sidney inserted before Miles could reply.

"I do not believe—"

Sidney held up a hand to stop Miles from speaking. "After all, you have taught us all that certain people are beneath our notice."

Miles glared at his brother, who merely smiled in

return as he held Miles's gaze while he continued to speak. "I would assume that Miles is only saving you from having to exert yourself in attempting to show even a modicum of decency in greeting them."

Miles's mouth dropped open. That was precisely what he was doing, but the fact that his brother had figured it out was not what was shocking. No, the incredulous part of what Sidney said was the fact that he never spoke against their father. He had always bent one way or the other to please their father. However, the look Sidney wore said he was unwilling to be swayed by anything today.

"Father is here to attempt to persuade you to consider breaking off your engagement with Miss Wesley to be his heir in my place," Sidney explained.

"He is?" That would explain Sidney's disgruntled air, though it did raise a few other questions. "He is not here because of the article in the paper?"

"What article in the paper?" Sir Allen looked appropriately confused. The news about the news story must not have reached him yet.

Whether it was proper or not to do so, Miles

found a touch of pleasure in throwing this punch at his father. "The one that says my great grandmother was a lady of the night."

His father blanched, and for the first time in Miles's life, his father seemed to deflate before him. Apparently, the article was not a fabrication, for if it were, Sir Allen would have reddened with rage and begun bellowing.

"Augusta." The name was more breathed than spoken. It must have been Aunt Augusta who had shared the story with the paper.

"Our great grandmother was what?"

Miles turned to his shocked brother. "Our great grandfather's mistress and pregnant when they wed. I can assure you that I was as surprised as you when I heard it."

Sidney chuckled. "And he wishes to tell us whom to marry? As if our selections could be worse than that!" He shook his head and continued to chuckle softly while looking excessively amused.

So, it must be Sidney's selection of bride that made him unacceptable as their father's heir. However... "I thought you were courting a Sir Allen-approved lady."

"I was until Lucy – Miss Gibbs – decided she would rather marry someone with a better title and income."

"My condolences."

"Do not be concerned on my behalf, little brother. Lucy was a touch above herself, which I would imagine is why father dearest liked her so much. I am relieved to be rid of her. My heart's choice is less father-approved."

A sound very like a grunt came from Sir Allen. "A Chapman marries for position."

"Great Grandfather did not," Sidney argued.

Miles shook his head. "I do not understand. If Father is attempting to replace you with me, why did he bring you with him?"

"That would be so that you could see the humiliation which refusing to follow his directives brings."

Miles's head snapped backward at that. "Did he think he had not already demonstrated such a thing to me? Do you know what he has done to me? To Charlotte?"

Sidney shrugged and nodded.

"It is the other way around," Sir Allen declared. "You, I have already dismissed," he said to Miles.

Well, that did make more sense. Miles looked at the lady beside him and then at her father. He smiled as he realized just how ridiculous his father's plan was. The outrageousness of presenting what Miles had as something to be avoided buoyed his confidence. He took Charlotte's hand and lifted it to his lips.

"Allow me to assist Father and present the terrible future you could face if you do not do as he wishes." Sarcasm dripped from his tone, causing his father to redden with anger. Miles did not care. His father had cast him aside and treated Charlotte abominably. Just as he had told Mrs. Wesley the other morning, Sir Allen deserved to be knocked around a bit so he could feel some of what he had, in his arrogance, inflicted on others.

"As you can see, Sidney, I am in a position not to be desired. For, I have been welcomed into a family of some means even though they know my fortune is nearly nothing. I have a sensible and pretty lady who has accepted my hand, not because she seeks to better her position or to gain more pin money than she would elsewhere, but because she loves me." He smiled at Charlotte. "And whom I love dearly." He turned back to his brother. "I will have to take up a profession, but I have already secured a position as a research assistant to a doctor of some renown in Bath, who happens to be married to our sister. As I am certain you can tell, my lot in life is dire, and it is fully due to the fact that I refused to abandon my heart, despite our father's cries that my tying myself to this family was beneath a Chapman."

Sidney grinned widely. "I shudder to think such a dreadful lot could befall me, but it does appear to be what my future holds."

"You have always done my bidding," Sir Allen snapped at Sidney.

"Yes, I have."

"And you." He turned toward Miles. "I have required very little of you."

"No," Miles retorted, "you required something of great significance, but I will not give her up."

Sir Allen flew to his feet. "You would choose some no-account piece of linen over a baronetcy?"

Miles stood and took a step toward his father. "Yes. And I will not have you speak so about her."

"She has relations who were in trade."

"And I have a great grandmother who was a doxie! At least, the Wesleys sold proper goods."

Rage flamed in Sir Allen's eyes as he turned away from his youngest son and toward Sidney. "Do you see what the wrong woman can do to a fellow? She can cause him to forget who he is and what is important."

Sidney turned his eyes to Miles and shook his head. "I believe, Father, that you mean she can help him realize what is truly valuable."

"A title and an estate are valuable." Sir Allen's chest lifted and lowered in great deliberate breaths.

"Not as valuable as a heart," Sidney retorted. "But what would you know of that? You have none."

"Be careful what you say, son," Sir Allen snarled.

Sidney folded his arms and met his father's glare with one of his own. Miles would have never thought that his brother, who lived to please, would be his source of support in confronting their father, and even if he had, he would never have imagined that Sidney possessed such boldness.

"To whom am I to leave my estate if neither of you will oblige me?" Sir Allen demanded.

"Perhaps there is a distant cousin?" Miles suggested. If Sidney could rise to the occasion on

Miles's behalf, it was only right and proper that the aid be repaid.

"Yes, I believe there is," Sidney said. "Some fellow in the former colonies." He rubbed his chin. "I cannot remember his name."

"I am not leaving my estate to some American!"

"There is Judith's husband," Miles offered. It was delightfully fun to have the upper hand in this discussion. It was even better than the discussion he had witnessed at Belle's wedding breakfast, for his father was, presently, in a more precarious position.

"He would sell it to buy one of his daughters a horse," Sir Allen snapped.

There was no love lost between Judith's husband and Sir Allen for Judith had married a man of means and sense who loved his wife and daughters more than anything and was intent upon leaving them well-provided-for when he was gone.

Sir Allen huffed. "I suppose it will fall to Henrietta to marry well."

"No!" Sidney cried.

Sir Allen's smile was cunningly evil. "You can prevent it."

"I do not see how," Sidney answered, "for I will

neither give up the lady I love nor will I allow you to badger our sister into marrying someone she does not love."

"If that is your choice, then you cannot stop me from seeing my estate settled on a proper husband for your sister." Sir Allen straightened his coat sleeves and looked excessively pleased with himself. "Neither of you are my sons any longer." He turned toward the door. "I shall have my solicitor remove you from my will as soon as I am home."

Sidney moved to follow his father from the room, but Sir Allen stopped and turned toward him. "I do not provide transportation to strangers. I shall have your things removed from the carriage. Do with them what you will."

"Father, you cannot be serious," Sidney said.

"You are welcome to stay with us," Mr. Wesley inserted. "I have carriages enough to see that you are taken home when you wish."

"Carriages, you say?" Sir Allen looked at Mr. Wesley with some interest.

"Yes, and servants enough to spare those needed to make the journey a comfortable one." Mr. Wesley placed himself between Sir Allen and Sidney. Apparently, Mr. Wesley did not limit his goodness and protection to just those gentlemen who wanted to marry his daughter.

"Indeed?" Sir Allen assessed the man before him.

"And connections enough to see that both Miles and his brother are safely settled into their futures. Did you receive Mr. Eyers' letter?"

Sir Allen's eyes narrowed. "I did."

"Then, you know my words are not without weight."

"That was your doing?"

"It was." He turned away from Sir Allen. "Mr. Chapman, would you care to be our guest? I assure you that it is no imposition. We have rooms that are rarely used, and it will be a delight to not have them vacant."

"I would be grateful for the use of one for a day or two," Sidney answered.

"Well, then, that is settled." Mr. Wesley pushed past Sir Allen and poked his head out into the hallway. "Hillier, see that Mr. Chapman's things are removed from Sir Allen's carriage and that a room is prepared for him right away. Perhaps the one adjoining Miles's room would be best."

"Shall I inform Mrs. Wesley?"

"Please. She will see that anything else which needs doing is done."

"Sir Allen," he said with a nod and a wave of his hand toward the door. "I would say it was a pleasure to meet you, but it was not. However, your sons seem to be worthy of my notice. I know Miles is."

Miles's father sucked in a quick breath through his nose – a sure sign that he was insulted. The thought was somewhat satisfying even if watching his father turn his back on him and Sidney was painful.

"It is you," Sir Allen spat at Charlotte. "You with your charms and allurements. You have done this." He took a step towards her. "Enticing little temptress!"

"That is enough!" Mr. Wesley cried. "You will leave my home at once."

"He will grow to hate you," Sir Allen snarled.

"No, he will not." Miles grabbed his father by the left arm. "Mr. Wesley asked you to leave."

"What is he to me?"

Clearly, something inside his father's mind had snapped.

"He is the owner of this house." Sidney had

taken his father's right arm. "And he has asked you to leave." He tipped his head toward the door, and Miles nodded.

Sir Allen continued his diatribe of unpleasantness as his sons forced him from the room and out of the house.

Two men were quickly unloading Sidney's few bags from the carriage as Sir Allen entered the vehicle, shouting for his driver to drive on.

"Do not leave until the luggage has been removed," Miles said to the driver.

"But the master..."

"Drive on!" Sir Allen shouted as he stuck his head out of the carriage door. "I do not care if he has his things. Drive on, I say! Drive..." He grimaced. "On." His face pinched in pain.

"Father!" Sidney cried as Sir Allen fell from the carriage, his body hitting the pavement first and then his head bouncing on impact with the ground.

"Roll him over," Miles said. "Does he breathe?"

Blood trickled from Sir Allen's ear as Sidney rolled him over and placed his ear near his father's mouth. "I do not hear any breath."

Miles laid his ear against Sir Allen's chest. He

strained to hear a heartbeat. There was nothing. He opened his father's coat and unbuttoned his waistcoat. Again, he pressed his ear against Sir Allen's chest. Still, there was nothing to hear. There was nothing to feel.

"Do you hear anything?"

He looked up at Sidney and shook his head.

"Is he dead?"

Miles nodded.

Sidney expelled a breath as if someone had punched him in the stomach. It was very much the way Miles was feeling.

"He is dead."

"He is," Miles said. The man who had controlled his life for so long lay in front of him unable to draw a breath or will his heart to beat. His power was gone. Completely.

"I should feel sad," Sidney muttered. "But, I do not. At least, not very."

Miles shook his head. "Neither do I. Perhaps with time?"

Sidney shrugged. "Perhaps."

But as time progressed over the course of that day and into the next, no deep sadness over-whelmed Miles except when he thought of his mother. It was for her that he cried, for she had seemed to truly care for his father. However, for the man himself, Miles could not cry. He could feel regret. He could feel remorse. He could even feel a sense of loss. He just could not feel sorrow.

"Please visit," Sidney said when he stood next to the Chapman carriage two days later after having seen that a letter and his father's body were on their way back to the Chapman estate.

"I will come when the will is to be read."

"Excellent. Mother will be so pleased to see you, and I know she will love Miss Wesley when she finally gets to meet her."

Tears gathered as Miles thought once again about his mother. However, these were tears of joy because he would be allowed to see her again. "Give her my love."

"I will." And with that, Sir Sidney, the new baronet Chapman, entered his carriage.

Miles stood on the driveway, watching the carriage until it had entered the road. Then, he turned and looked at the face of the Wesleys' house with its flat front and neat windows. While he looked forward to being able to see his mother again, he did not think of the place where he grew up as home. His home stood at the door, waiting for him to return to her. Wherever Charlotte was, that would always be his home.

~*~*~

And a happy home it would be. Charlotte and Miles would never want for love or finances. He would finish his term and pass his exams. They would marry and set up a fine home in Bath, for Miles had never been written out of his father's will and his inheritance was not insignificant. However, despite his fortune, he would still choose to work alongside his brother-in-law, helping him write papers and publish books. His children – both his two sons and his one daughter – would adore him, nearly as much as their mother did, and he would be thought of and spoken about as what he had longed to be, a good man.

Much of that was still to occur on the day two years later when Miles stood next to Tom at the front of a chapel near the Wesley's estate, listening to the parson read the wedding service for Tom and Louisa just as he had done a year earlier for Miles and Charlotte.

Charlotte sat behind Miles, holding a precious little bundle named Wesley Lewis Chapman, their first child, for Louisa had insisted that her name-sake be present at her wedding. No matter how many times Charlotte told her sister that Wesley was not Louisa's namesake but rather that of their father, Louisa would not listen. She doted on Wesley, or Lou, as she insisted on calling him, and Miles worried that the child might end up spoiled at his aunt's hand. However, Charlotte assured him that it was a worry that need not be entertained because sensible ladies did not have spoiled children.

He winked at her as the parson asked them to kneel for prayer, causing her to arch an eyebrow which said he should be paying attention to the service instead of her – even if her smile said she enjoyed the attention. As he took his place and the minister read the words in the prayer book, Miles cast one more appreciative look at his wife. Then, bowing his head, he said his own prayer of thanks for the twisted path through misdeeds, injury, and vicious lies that had led him to her, his beautiful, sensible heart.

# Before You Go

If you enjoyed this book, be sure to let others know by leaving a review.

~*~*~

Want to know when other books in this series will be available?
You can always know what's new with my books by subscribing to my mailing list.
(There will, of course, be a thank you gift for joining because I think my readers are awesome!)
Book News from Leenie Brown
(bit.ly/LeenieBBookNews)

~*~*~

Turn the page to read an excerpt from another one of Leenie's books

## Other Pens Excerpt

[Have you ever wondered what happened to Henry Crawford after *Mansfield Park* ended? How about his sister or Tom Bertram? What about his friends who were never at Mansfield Park? If you have wondered about such things, you'll want to read my *Other Pens, Mansfield Park* series, which mixes Jane Austen's classic characters with a cast of original ones in situations never found in one of Miss Austen's novels. Below is an excerpt from the second book in the series, *Charles: To Discover His Purpose*, a story about how Henry Crawford's rakish friend Charles Edwards finds his happily ever after while attempting to steal a kiss.]

### CHAPTER 1

Charles Edwards squinted into the late afternoon sun – it was an action that he could almost do without any discomfort. The swelling around his eye had subsided, and soon, the bruising would fade to a nasty yellow and then disappear. Until that happened, he would continue to take his rides by wandering from one street to the next rather than face the taunting and questioning looks he was guaranteed to receive in the parks.

While it was an excellent way to avoid censure from his peers, it was dashed boring trotting up and down streets without so much as a single friend with whom to converse. Had he earned his scars more gallantly, perhaps he would not feel the need to hide them. To have been injured in a boxing match or defense of some lady's honor would make his bruises more of a badge than a blemish. However, since everyone in town had likely read that blasted article in the paper, the raised eyebrows from overprotective matrons and giggles from their charges would be unbearable. And then, there would be the gentlemen. He shook his head. Had he received a blackened eye from Trefor Linton for actually doing something inappropriate with Linton's sister, Constance, his friends would just laugh and clap him on the shoulder before filling his glass with some libation at his club.

But, he had not been caught doing anything improper. In fact, it was much worse than just not being found dallying with a debutante. He had been attempting to be gallant. He would do his best not to be put in such a situation again! Honourable actions and favours to ladies who were offering none in return must be avoided, for they only led to broken noses, disgrace, and lonely rambles up less well-to-do streets.

"Mr. Edwards?"

Charles drew his horse to a stop just in front of a carriage that was standing at the ready to receive a lovely young woman. He had not bothered to take note of her since this was not the part of town where the finest flowers of the season resided.

"Miss Linton," he said doffing his hat. "Is Crawford with you?" He nodded to the carriage.

"No," Constance Linton replied with a smile, "though he very much wanted to be. It is just Evelyn and I."

His brows furrowed. Evelyn? The name sounded familiar.

"Miss Barrett," Constance clarified.

"Ah, Miss Barrett. Of course. How negligent of me to not remember." How had he managed to forget her name? He certainly had not forgotten her perfectly pink lips or lithe figure...the same figure that was exiting the house to his left. She was perhaps the most enticing creature he had ever met and never sampled.

"Oh!"

Miss Barrett's lips formed such a wonderfully kissable o.

"Mr. Edwards," she greeted with a small curtsey. "Are you here to visit Mrs. Verity and the children?"

His brows furrowed again. "Mrs. Who?"

"Verity," Evelyn repeated. "She runs this home for children." She motioned toward the house.

"I did not know this was a home for children." His left brow rose in question. "Why are you here? None of these children are yours, I would assume."

Her eyes grew wide, and she gasped. "We are not all as reprobate as you, Mr. Edwards."

He leaned forward, nonchalantly admiring her look of utter indignation. "Then, what, pray tell, are proper young ladies such as yourself and Miss Linton doing here?"

"Charitable work. You do know what that is, do you not?"

He chuckled. Miss Barret was not the sort to shy away quietly to her corner and leave him be. He liked that. "I have heard the term."

"But have you ever experienced it?" asked Constance.

He shifted his gaze to his friend, Henry Crawford's, betrothed. "No, not beyond what is expected on my father's estate."

"It's rather fulfilling," Constance replied. "Today, we taught some children their letters. It was remarkable, was it not, Evelyn?" She wore a look of sheer delight.

"And Linton approves of this?" Charles asked.

"Both he and Henry do."

Delight did not begin to describe the look in Miss Linton's eyes as she said the name Henry. One day, when he was ready to take up his mantle of responsibility, Charles hoped to find a lady who would look even half as happy saying his name as Miss Linton did at this moment.

"Trefor," Constance continued, "thought this would be a safe way to keep me occupied. My last scheme, you see, did not leave him favourably disposed to allowing me to find ways in which to make my life more interesting."

There was a mischievous gleam in both her eyes and those of her friend Evelyn. Curious, that. He had not expected anything akin to impishness from Trefor Linton's sister or any of her friends. Constance Linton was the most proper chit he had ever met, and he suspected, to be her friend, Miss Barrett must be the same.

"Is your eye feeling better?" Miss Barrett asked.

"It is, but I'll not be doing either of you any favours in the future," he replied with a smirk. "At least not unless I receive something better than a broken nose and a black eye in return."

"I can neither apologize or thank you enough," Constance replied.

She had apologized over and over and over again as she stood holding a compress to his eye in the Linton sitting room those many days ago. "I think you have said the words enough," he replied softly. "I merely jest." He would not have her feeling guilty for his injuries when it was not her doing which caused them.

Miss Barrett tipped her head as she looked up at him, a puzzled look on her face. Then, she shook herself and smiled. "We are expected at your house soon, Connie. Mother will be waiting."

"As will Trefor," she smiled, "and Henry."

Much to Charles's surprise, Miss Evelyn Barrett rolled her eyes at the tone her friend used to say Henry's name.

"Do not let me detain you. I would not wish to run afoul of any of them." He winked at Miss Barret. "At least, not until I am healed."

She gasped. "My mother has warned me about you, Mr. Edwards."

"As well she should," he replied easily. "I am dreadfully charming."

Constance had entered the carriage, but Evelyn, who remained on the street, laughed. "That is not how my mother said it." Her eyes sparkled with impertinence. Then, with a small curtsey of parting, she boarded her carriage.

Charles looked after her and tipped his hat as the door closed on those shining eyes and teasing smile. Oh, he could find great pleasure in evoking such a look from her on a regular basis. Not that he wished to spend great amounts of time with her. No, he was not the sort of gentleman to trot around behind a lady hoping for her to smile at him or laugh at his jokes. He danced; he flirted; and he stole kisses. He did not become attached. Attachments were dangerous. They led to marriage and, he fought the urge to shudder, responsibility. He was far too young for such things as that just yet.

Still, he wondered where she would be this evening and if there would be any dark corners into which she might be persuaded.

He blew out a breath. Hiding himself away from society was perhaps not the best idea in the world. It apparently was wreaking havoc on his well-ordered, carefree existence. A rogue such as himself did not stalk his prey. He simply looked for the opportunity and took it. Planning anything was far too much like being responsible. Rules, guidelines, ledgers, accounts, and all the rest that went with being a gentleman of standing belonged to his father, not Charles.

In front of him, the carriage stopped, a man jumped down, the door opened, and a pretty face peered out, looking back to where he was.

He nudged his horse forward as Miss Barrett waved him towards her.

"Do you require help?" he asked as he drew near.

"No, no, we are well. Connie and I were just talking, and I thought as we were discussing how dreadful it is that you were injured on Connie's account that it would be charitable of us to offer you a place in the Linton's box at the theatre tonight."

Charles began to shake his head.

"Hear me out. Do not refuse until I have made my full request. And come forward more, I feel as if I am going to fall out of this door and onto the street."

Charles chuckled. This young woman sounded more like Linton's cantankerous Aunt Gwladys than a young lady of the ton. Most young ladies who presented themselves during the season went out of their way to appear demure to one and all – always.

"Do you scold everyone?" he teased as he did as she said.

If he had expected her to be offended, he was once again going to be surprised, for she merely smiled, batted her lashes, and replied, "No, I scold very few beyond my brother actually."

"So, I am special," he returned.

She shrugged. "Perhaps you are. Or perhaps I just find you as troublesome as Griffin."

"I think I will insist you find me special."

"Do what you will; it matters not one jot to me," she retorted.

Her words might have said she did not care, but her tone clearly said she was annoyed.

"As I was saying..."

"Before you began scolding." Charles smiled at her huff.

"Before I had to pause to give instructions."

Charles chuckled. "Continue. I shall not refuse until you have said your piece."

"Refuse? You intend to refuse?"

"Most likely. But, I have not heard your request in full, so I cannot be certain I am correct until I do. I have been wrong before."

Her brows rose, and her lips pursed for a moment as if she were holding back some retort.

"There will not be very many people in our box. If you slip in a side door or something and scurry up to the box, you will not have to have many people gawk at you."

"You think I am worried about being seen?"

"I would be if my eye were the colour of yours. That *is* why you are riding here and not in a more populated place, is it not? And, I have not seen you at any events since...well..." she pointed to her eye.

"I will admit that I do not relish the whispers." Why he felt he needed to admit such a thing was beyond him. He could come up with any number of reasons to be riding where he was and for not having been at any soiree she had attended. A smile slipped slowly across his face. "Have you missed me?"

"What?" She shook her head vigorously. "No. I just noticed that I had not seen you slinking from shadow to shadow."

"If you say so."

"I do." She scowled. "Now, will you be joining us? I am certain no one would be in the least put out if you did."

"How reassuring," Charles muttered.

"Please," Constance added from the interior of the carriage. "I do feel dreadful that you have been out of society. It must be terribly boring sitting at home instead of going out."

"Who said I was sitting at home?" He smiled a lazy, suggestive smile.

"Henry," Constance replied.

Blast! Did Henry tell her everything?

"Very well, I have been hiding away. Are you happy to know my shame?"

"Only if it means you will join us," said Miss Barrett.

"Can you not muster an ounce of sympathy?" he asked in surprise. Were not young ladies – especially those who did charity work – supposed to be compassionate?

She shook her head. "No. Not a morsel. While I am awfully sorry you were injured, I do believe you have escaped more times than you have been caught."

The lady might look like an angel, but she had a heart of ice. However, ice could be melted. In fact, it could be quite a marvelous lark to attempt to melt that ice.

"Very well, I will join you if you will but attempt to feel an ounce of pity for me."

The way her lips pursed with contained amusement was tempting. "A full ounce?"

"Yes." He moved closer to her door. "A full ounce." He repeated the words in a low, sultry tone – slowly and deliberately. Satisfaction curled his lips as he saw her pretty nibble-worthy neck rise and fall when she swallowed.

She licked her lips. "I shall make an attempt."

"Then, I shall see you at the theatre."

"Very good."

He chuckled at the uncertainty in her voice. Again, he tipped his hat to the closed carriage door and watched it drive away before continuing on his way home to prepare for an evening of entertainment – and a play.

# Acknowledgements

There are many who have had a part in the creation of this story. Some have read and commented on it. Some have proofread for grammatical errors and plot holes. Others have not even read the story, and a few, I know, never will. However, their encouragement and belief in my ability, as well as their patience when I became cranky or when supper was late or the groceries ran low, was invaluable.

And so, I would like to say *thank you* to Zoe, Rose, Kristine, Ben, and Kyle, as well as my Sweet Tuesday readers on Patreon and my blog, who followed this story as it developed and waited, as patiently as one might do, from one Tuesday to the next, to read a new chapter. I feel blessed through your help, support, and understanding.

I have not listed my dear husband in the above group because, to me, he deserves his own special thank you, for, without his somewhat pushy insistence that I start sharing my writing, none of my writing goals and dreams would have been met.

# Other Leenie B Books

You can find all of Leenie's books at this link
bit.ly/LeenieBBooks
where you can explore the collections below

~*~

Other Pens

~*~

Touches of Austen Collection

~*~

Nature's Fury and Delights, Novelette Anthologies

~*~

Sweet Possibilities and Sweet Extras

~*~

Dash of Darcy and Companions Collection

~*~

Marrying Elizabeth Series

~*~

Willow Hall Romances

~*~

The Choices Series

~*~

Darcy Family Holidays

~*~

Teatime Tales Novelettes Collection

~*~

Darcy and... An Austen-Inspired Collection

## About the Author

Leenie Brown has always been a girl with an active imagination, which, while growing up, was both an asset, providing many hours of fun as she played out stories, and a liability, when her older sister and aunt would tell her frightening tales. At one time, they had her convinced Dracula lived in the trunk at the end of the bed she slept in when visiting her grandparents!

Although it has been years since she cowered in her bed in her grandparents' basement, she still has an imagination which occasionally runs away with her, and she feeds it now as she did then — by reading!

Her heroes, when growing up, were authors, and the worlds they painted with words were (and still are) her favourite playgrounds! Now, as an adult, she spends much of her time in the Regency world, playing with the characters from her favourite Jane Austen novels and those of her own creation.

When she is not traipsing down a trail in an attempt to keep up with her imagination, Leenie resides in the beautiful province of Nova Scotia with her two sons and her very own Mr. Brown (a wonderful mix of all the best of Darcy, Bingley, and Edmund with a healthy dose of the teasing Mr. Tilney and just a dash of the scolding Mr. Knightley).

# Connect with Leenie

*E-mail:*
*LeenieBrownAuthor@gmail.com*
*Facebook:*
www.facebook.com/LeenieBrownAuthor
*Blog:*
*leeniebrown.com*
*Patreon:*
https://www.patreon.com/LeenieBrown
*Subscribe to Leenie's Mailing List:*
Book News from Leenie Brown
(bit.ly/LeenieBBookNews)